"Beth, I don't want to scare you, but I thought you should know that I might have brought danger to you."

A hardness that had been around his heart cracked apart and fell away. "That means I don't want you staying here alone. That means I don't even want you out of my sight."

If somebody was after her because they thought she was his lover, there was no real way to disabuse them of that notion. He'd already made her a target and the best he could hope for was that he could keep her safe until he returned to Barajas.

But for tonight he didn't intend to go anywhere. And all he could think about was that they had been damned by what they weren't doing—so why not go ahead and do it? Why not become her lover?

He stood once again and took her by the hand and pulled her up from her chair.

"The coffee is ready," she murmured as he drew her into his arms.

"Hmm, suddenly I'm not in the mood for coffee." He leaned down and touched his lips to the warm flesh of her neck, then nibbled at the skin just beneath her ear. He felt the quickened beat of her heart against his and a faint tremor that stole through her. "I think it's time I made good on that earlier promise."

She didn't ask what promise he was talking about; rather she drew a shuddery breath and took him by the hand and led him down the hall toward her bedroom.

CARLA CASSIDY

BY ORDER OF THE PRINCE

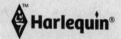

TORONTO NEW YORK LONDON
AMSTERDAM PARIS SYDNEY HAMBURG
STOCKHOLM ATHENS TOKYO MILAN MADRID
PRAGUE WARSAW BUDAPEST AUCKLAND

Special thanks and acknowledgment to Carla Cassidy for her contribution to the Cowboys Royale series.

Recycling programs
for this product may
not exist in your area.

ISBN-13: 978-0-373-74608-8

BY ORDER OF THE PRINCE

ABOUT THE AUTHOR

Carla Cassidy is an award-winning author who has written more than fifty novels for Harlequin Books. In 1995, she won Best Silhouette Romance from *RT Book Reviews* for *Anything for Danny*. In 1998, she also won a Career Achievement Award for Best Innovative Series from *RT Book Reviews*.

Carla believes the only thing better than curling up with a good book to read is sitting down at the computer with a good story to write. She's looking forward to writing many more books and bringing hours of pleasure to readers.

Books by Carla Cassidy

HARLEQUIN INTRIGUE

1077—THE SHERIFF'S SECRETARY
1114—PROFILE DURANGO
1134—INTERROGATING THE BRIDE+
1140—HEIRESS RECON+
1146—PREGNESIA+
1175—SCENE OF THE CRIME: BRIDGEWATER, TEXAS
1199—ENIGMA
1221—WANTED: BODYGUARD
1258—SCENE OF THE CRIME: BACHELOR MOON
1287—BY ORDER OF THE PRINCE

+The Recovery Men

CAST OF CHARACTERS

Beth Taylor—This hardworking beauty is drawn into danger by a handsome prince.

Prince Antoine Cavanaugh—He's determined to find out what happened to his friend and is unable to stay away from the pretty housekeeper, Beth.

Sheikh Amir Khalid—A bomb destroyed his car, but his body was never found. Where is the sheikh and who is behind the attack?

Jake Wolf—Sheriff of Wind River. Can the lawman be trusted?

Michael Napolis—Head of Security for Prince Antoine. Is he part of a bigger conspiracy?

Aleksei Verovick—Tied to the Russian mob. Is he behind the attacks on the royals?

Chapter One

It was creepy—packing away the personal belongings of a guest who nobody knew was dead or alive. Beth Taylor, head of housekeeping at the luxury Wind River Ranch and Resort, unlocked the door to one of the exclusive plush suites and pushed it open.

Just a little over three weeks had passed since Sheik Amir Khalid, one of the royals who had come to the hotel for a meeting, had gotten into a limo that had driven a short distance and then blown up. The driver had been killed, but nobody knew what had happened to Amir. The only witness to the event had seen the sheik crawl out of the wreckage and he'd been picked up by somebody. The problem was nobody knew if it had been friend or foe who had picked up the injured man.

"It's time to clear the room," Beth's boss had said to her minutes earlier. "It's been three weeks with no word and I can't hold the room forever. I'd like you to personally take care of it, Beth. We'll lock up the belongings in storage until somebody comes to claim them."

And so here she was, in a room where Sheik Amir Khalid had checked in as part of a four-nation coalition who had come here to discuss trade agreements that would benefit their individual countries. She pulled the luggage caddy she'd brought with her into the room and closed the door behind her.

The tasteful opulence of these suites never failed to amaze her. The thick carpeting beneath her feet, the subtle touches of gold trim in the woodwork and the oversized furniture all whispered of a kind of wealth Beth couldn't even begin to imagine.

Immediately after high school, Beth, who'd had a sickly mother to care for, had gotten a job as maid at the resort. Three years ago, after eight years of working hard, she'd finally been promoted to head of housekeeping, an often difficult but rewarding job.

She fought the impulse to kick off her high heels, peel off her pantyhose and dig her toes into the plush rug. Instead she headed for the bedroom. The king-size bed was truly fit for a king, with a rich navy bedspread and matching draperies that could either be drawn against the sun or opened to display the beautiful view of the Wyoming landscape.

Sheik Amir hadn't even spent a single night before the explosion had occurred, but his clothing had been neatly hung in the closet.

Her fingers lingered over the rich silks and other expensive fabrics as she carefully folded them and returned them to the suitcase she found on the floor in the closet.

With the closet once again empty she moved to the bathroom and quickly packed the personal grooming items that were scattered on the counter.

What had happened to Amir? It was the question on everyone's lips. Had he managed to get out of the limo alive only to be picked up by enemies and then killed? The area had been searched but no clues had been found to solve the mystery of the missing sheik.

Returning to the bedroom she beelined for the nightstands. Although she didn't think the sheik had been in the bedroom long enough to place anything inside the drawers, she wanted to be thorough.

The nightstands were tall and ornate, with marble tops and heavy drawers. She went to the one on the far side of the bed first. As she pulled open the top drawer she found herself thinking about how crazy everything had gotten since the dark-haired handsome sheik had taken the limo ride and never returned.

For the past three weeks the hotel had been turned upside down with the arrival of the royals. Reporters had flooded the area and there had even been local protests about the trade agreements. Since Amir's disappearance the air had grown even more intense as the various security teams scrambled to make sure the remaining leaders stayed safe.

With a shake of her head she focused on the task at hand. The nightstand drawers held nothing that belonged to Sheik Amir so she moved to the ones on the near side of the bed.

She gasped as she pulled the top drawer out too far and it fell to the floor. "Darn," she muttered, hoping she hadn't marred the beautiful wood. As she picked it up to put it back, she felt something odd on the bottom.

Frowning, she flipped the empty drawer over to see what her fingers had encountered. A white envelope was taped to the bottom. She stared at it in confusion as her heart stepped up its rhythm.

What was it? Had another guest at one time or another taped it there? Or had Sheik Amir wanted to hide something before he'd left the room for the night? There was only one way to tell.

She wasn't sure why but her fingers trembled slightly as she pulled the envelope from the drawer. It wasn't sealed. She pulled out the papers folded inside and opened them.

Her heart banged against her chest and a gasp escaped her as she saw the words printed on the first page.

DEATH WILL COME BEFORE YOU SEE SUCCESS WITH THE COIN COALITION.

She quickly scanned the next note.

BETRAYERS ALL OF YOU AND THE PRICE OF BETRAYAL IS DEATH.

There were a total of five and they were all threats to the visiting royals.

There was no question that the envelope had been placed there by Sheik Amir Khalid. COIN was the name of the partnership of the four Mediterranean nations led by the men who had arrived to make their trade agreements with the United States.

Had the person who had written the notes managed to achieve the goal of killing the sheik? And it was obvious from the notes that he hadn't been the only target. All members of COIN had been threatened.

She needed to take the notes to Jake Wolf, the sheriff of Wind River County. He'd know what to do with them and maybe could glean some clues from the content that would point to the person behind the threats.

Her fingers still shook as she carefully put the notes back into the envelope and then shoved it into her skirt pocket. She bent down to put the drawer back into place and then stood with a deep sigh.

"Excuse me."

She squealed in surprise and whirled around at the sound of the deep male voice coming from behind her. Her heart tap-danced in her chest at the sight of Prince Antoine Cavanaugh.

She wasn't sure if her heart beat even faster because the envelope suddenly burned like fire in her pocket or if it was because the prince was the hottest-looking man she'd ever seen in her entire life.

"I was passing Amir's room and thought I heard somebody inside. I decided to come in and investigate." His pale blue eyes gazed around the room and then narrowed slightly as he looked back at her.

She felt a flush working up from the pit of her stomach to warm her face. From the moment she'd seen him, with his neatly cut light brown hair and those light blue eyes against his delicious dark olive skin, she'd felt a ridiculous teenage flutter in the pit of her stomach.

His white long-sleeved dress shirt fit perfectly across his broad shoulders and the black slacks he wore emphasized his slim hips. Even from this distance she could smell him, a wonderful blend of exotic spicy cologne that could dizzy her brain if she allowed it.

She suddenly realized she was staring at him and had yet to find her tongue to respond.

"Prince Antoine, I'm Beth Taylor, head of housekeeping," she began.

He nodded. "Yes, I know who you are,

Ms. Taylor. I see you're packing up Amir's things. Has there been word about him that I haven't heard?"

"No, nothing like that."

"Then I don't suppose you found anything that might provide a clue as to what happened to him?"

The envelope in her skirt seemed to burn hotter. "No," she said quickly. "No, I didn't find anything like that. I'm just packing his things so we can move them to storage, but I didn't find anything. Unfortunately we can't hold this room forever. We have other guests to think about."

His eyes narrowed slightly. "When you finish in here would you mind coming to my room? I have something I'd like to discuss with you." Those blue eyes of his seemed to pierce right through her and her first instinct was to tell him she had other things to do. But she valued her job and the last person she wanted to upset was one of the visiting royals. She could just imagine having to tell her boss that she blew off

Prince Antoine because he made her more than a little bit weak in the knees.

"Of course," she replied briskly. "It should only take me a few more minutes to finish up in here."

"Then I'll expect you in a few minutes." He gave her a curt nod and then turned on his heels and left the room.

Beth drew a deep breath, realizing that while he'd been standing there she'd scarcely breathed. The man wasn't just a royal prince, he was royal sin walking.

She hadn't missed the way other women in the hotel followed his movements with hungry gazes whenever he and his security team made an appearance. Antoine and his twin brother, Sebastian, had definitely been a special form of eye candy for the other guests.

Sebastian had left a week ago to return to the country of Barajas where he and Antoine were co-rulers, but Antoine had remained here.

As she continued checking the room for anything else that belonged to Amir, she tried to calm her frazzled nerves. Prince Antoine probably wanted to talk to her about some housekeeping service that he thought wasn't up to par, or maybe he needed something that wasn't normally provided.

There was absolutely no reason to believe that he wanted to talk to her about what she'd found. He couldn't have known that she'd found anything and there was no way she was turning those notes over to anyone but Jake Wolf.

Still, as she walked through the suite one last time, she couldn't help the nervous tension that coiled in her stomach as she thought about facing Prince Antoine again.

"YOUR HIGHNESS, you worried me." Michael Napolis, the head of Antoine's security team, met him at the door as Antoine returned to his suite. Michael's bulldog features displayed more than a touch of reproach. "One minute you were here and the next minute you were gone."

"Relax, Michael. I just stepped across the

hall to speak to a member of hotel house-keeping. You can go to your own room now. I'm in for the rest of the night and will call you if I need you for anything."

"As you wish," Michael replied with a small nod of his big head, but it was obvious he wasn't happy. Antoine suspected that if Michael had his way he'd sleep on the floor next to Antoine's bed to keep him safe. Michael had been a nervous wreck since Amir's disappearance, at least giving the appearance that he was worried sick about Antoine.

Once Michael had left the suite Antoine sank into the large leather chair in front of the fireplace and stared unseeing at the neatly stacked unburned logs.

She'd lied.

Antoine had spent years in his country's military as one of the top interrogators. He'd been trained to find lies and break liars to get at the truth. The national security of Barajas had often depended on the information Antoine got from a particular prisoner.

There was no question in his mind that Beth Taylor had lied to him when he'd asked her if she'd found anything in Amir's room. He hadn't missed the subtle shift of her body weight away from him as she'd answered him, or the fact that she had expressed no real surprise at his question and instead had been far too verbose in her answer.

Bottom line—she'd lied, and Antoine was determined to find out what, exactly, she had found in his missing friend's room.

He looked toward the window where the sun had begun to make its descent. Another night would soon be upon them without answers about Amir. *Where are you, my friend? What has happened to you?*

With each day that passed, Antoine found himself growing more and more paranoid. He was unsure who to trust. Certainly not the local authorities, who had already proven to be untrustworthy. As much as he hated to admit it, he wasn't even sure he could trust his own security. It had only been a little over a week ago that Sheik Efraim Aziz, a fellow member of the coalition, had discovered that his own head of security had tried to kill him.

There were many people who had been unhappy with the COIN coalition's goals in working with the United States, many people who would love it if the COIN members simply disappeared.

Until a week ago he'd had his twin brother, the only person in the world he truly trusted, beside him, but Sebastian had gone back home where he belonged. He'd always been the stronger of the two when it came to the leadership of their small country. Barajas needed Sebastian and both the country and his brother would be fine without Antoine.

He glanced toward the door, surprised at the wing of anticipation that swept through him as he thought of Beth Taylor.

He'd noticed her the first day of his arrival. She'd been one of the hotel staff who had greeted him when they'd checked in. In that first moment he'd been struck by the soft curls of her shoulder-length blond hair, the bright green of her eyes and the lush fullness of her lips.

In the last three weeks of his stay here he'd seen her often, her long shapely legs moving her gracefully across the hotel lobby or down a hallway. But, other than enjoying the sight of her, he'd had no other interaction with her.

Now he wondered how easy she'd be to break. He'd definitely faced more daunting adversaries and yet had always managed to get what he wanted out of them.

As a soft knock sounded at the door, he rose from his chair, the sense of anticipation growing stronger. He checked through the security peephole and then opened the door.

"Thank you for coming," he said. She gave a curt nod but made no move to step over the threshold and into the room. "Please, come in." There was no way he intended to have this conversation standing in the doorway.

She walked past him and he caught the scent of her, a soft floral that reminded him of a field of wildflowers. It was viscerally appealing and he was vaguely surprised by his immediate response. He pointed her to the sofa. "Sit," he said.

He hadn't realized it sounded like a command until she jumped and quickly sank down on the very edge of the rich burgundy sofa. "Would you like something refreshing to drink?"

"No, thank you. I still have a lot of work to finish up before I can go home for the day."

He sat on the opposite end of the sofa and noticed that not only did she tense slightly, but her gaze surreptitiously swept over him before focusing quickly on her hands folded in her lap.

Interesting, he thought as he read her nonverbal clues. It was possible she was attracted to him. Good, he could use that bit of information in trying to get the truth from her.

"Do you have family waiting for you to get home?" he asked.

She shook her head, her blond curls looking achingly soft and touchable in the waning golden light that danced in through the window. "No, there's nobody waiting for me, but I like to get home before night falls." She gave an uncomfortable laugh. "Although that rarely happens."

"Especially now," he replied smoothly. He hadn't missed the slight wistfulness in her voice when she'd told him there was nobody waiting for her at home. "I'm sure our presence here has only increased the workload for the housekeeping staff, for you."

"Not really," she countered. "Our high standard of service goes out to each and every guest, whether they are a prince or an accountant."

There was a ring of pride in her voice. He liked that. His grandfather had always told him that it didn't matter what you did, as long as you did it well.

Assessing what he knew so far, he recognized that she was a beautiful woman who was probably lonely and had embraced her work to fill the voids in her life. It was information he would use to determine the best way to get her to confide in him.

"It's been a difficult couple of weeks," he said and saw the flash of sympathy that crossed her pretty features. "Amir was a good friend of mine. With what happened, I don't know who to trust anymore."

"We're all sick about how things have gone," she replied. She shifted positions, turning her knees in his direction. "I hope you're being very careful."

"It's difficult to be careful when you don't know in what form danger might come. I find myself feeling very isolated." He flashed her the smile that had charmed more than one woman in his lifetime. "I'm sorry to take up your time, I was just feeling a bit lonely and then I saw you and needed a moment of company."

Her cheeks blossomed with color and one of her hands shifted from her lap to touch the pocket in her skirt. His heart stepped up its beating. Whatever she'd found in Amir's room was now in her pocket. He was sure of it. Now all he had to do was get her to share it with him.

"I'm sure you know my brother returned to our country," he continued.

"Yes, it must have been difficult for you to remain behind."

He nodded. "But I don't intend to return until I know what happened to Amir. He was like a brother to me. Do you have brothers or sisters, Ms. Taylor?"

"No, I'm an only child." Now it was not only her knees that faced him, but her entire upper body, letting him know she was open to him, perhaps just a little bit vulnerable.

With cool calculation, he leaned toward her, nearly closing the distance between them. He lightly touched her shoulder. "I can't rest. I can't sleep until we find out something about Amir. The local officials have been little help with their issues of corruption. I'm desperate to find something, anything that might give me a clue as to what happened and who is to blame."

Once again her hand touched her pocket and he saw an uncertainty in the depths of her beautiful eyes. His heart seemed to stop beating as he waited for her reply.

"I did find something in Amir's room," she finally said. For a moment she remained perfectly still and Antoine was struck by a quicksilver desire to stroke a hand across the smooth skin of her sculpted cheek, taste the full lower lip she was now nibbling in obvious indecision. She reached into her pocket and pulled out an envelope, but didn't immediately offer it to Antoine.

"I found it taped on the bottom of a drawer in the bedroom. I was going to turn it over to Sheriff Wolf," she said. "But I guess it won't hurt if you look at it first." Her slender hand trembled slightly as she held out the envelope.

He took it, his heart once again rapping an unsteady beat as he opened it and withdrew the pieces of paper. He read the notes, electrified by the contents. "You read these?" he asked.

She nodded, her eyes wider than they had been minutes before. "They're terrible."

There was now no question in his mind

that the limo explosion had been meant to kill all of them, that it had been mere circumstance, a matter of sheer fate, that had placed Amir in that limo alone at the time of the bomb blast.

He placed the notes back in the envelope, but didn't return it to Beth. "Ms. Taylor, I have a favor to ask you. Please let me keep these and see what I can learn from them before you take them to Sheriff Wolf. I meant it when I told you I don't know who to trust."

She frowned thoughtfully. "What are you going to do?" she asked.

"A little investigating on my own, see if I can find out who is dirty and who isn't before I give these notes to anyone else."

Her frown deepened, the gesture doing nothing to detract from her beauty. "How are you going to be able to do that? You don't know any of the locals." She didn't wait for his response but instead continued, "You're going to need my help. I was born and raised here. I know the people who live here, and I also know the people who don't belong. The only way I'll give you the time you've asked for before going to Jake Wolf is if you let me help you."

She'd surprised him. The last thing he'd expected was her offer to partner up with him. His initial response was a resounding no, but there was no question that she could be useful.

"Okay, I accept your offer to help, but only on one condition—that if things get dangerous for you, then you step back."

"Agreed," she replied.

Antoine stuck out his hand and as they solemnly shook, he was aware of the softness of her skin against his, the delicate bones of her hands. A new flicker of something evocative and exciting swept through him. It had nothing to do with the fact that she might possibly be helpful to him in finding out who was behind the threats. Rather it was a flame of physical attraction.

"I've got to get back to work," she said as she quickly pulled her hand from his and stood.

"How much longer will you be?" he asked as they walked to the door.

She paused and looked at her watch. "Maybe another hour or so, why?"

"I'd like to make copies of these notes and then take them to somebody discreet and see if prints besides ours can be pulled from them, but I'm not sure where to go to get this done."

"Jane Cameron," she replied without hesitation.

He knew Jane Cameron was the forensic scientist who had been involved in processing the scene of the limo bombing. He also knew that she and Stefan Lutece, Prince of Kyros, had become involved in a romantic relationship. "And you trust Jane?"

"Absolutely," she replied. "Why don't I take the notes and make the copies in my office, then come back here when I'm finished for the day and we can go see Jane."

"Perfect," he replied. He gave her the envelope and then reached out to take her other hand in his. "I can't thank you enough for giving me some time to investigate this."

She squeezed his hand slightly and then pulled it away from him. "I just hope this isn't a mistake. I'll see you in about an hour." She flew through the door as if the hounds of hell were nipping at her heels.

Antoine closed the door behind her and tried to ignore the scent of her that lingered in the air. He was attracted to her like he hadn't been to a woman in a very long time.

There was something soft, something inviting about her that called to him. But, it was an attraction he had no desire to explore.

Antoine never allowed himself to get close to a woman. He could enjoy their company and have sex with them, but his heart never got involved.

He would do anything to find out who was behind the threats made on himself and the others. He would do anything to find out who had been behind the attack on Amir. If that meant using the pretty housekeeper, it wouldn't be the worst thing he'd ever done in his life.

Chapter Two

She had to be crazy.

Somehow between the time she'd left Amir's suite and the time she'd left Antoine's, she'd lost her ever-loving mind. The minute Beth reached her private office she sank down at her desk and shook her head, wondering what on earth she'd been thinking when she'd given Antoine that envelope, when she'd offered to help him.

She should have kept her mouth shut and taken the notes to Jake like she'd intended. The problem was she hadn't been thinking. Instead, she'd been falling into the blue depths of Antoine's eyes, touched by the loneliness and the feeling of isolation he hadn't tried to hide.

She'd offered her help because she'd

thought he needed it, which was a ridiculous thing for her to think. He was a prince, for God's sake. He had people to take care of his every wish, his every need. The last thing he needed was a simple woman who didn't know a thing about foreign politics and had only a high school education helping him investigate threats against members of royal families.

She checked her email and the voice mail on her phone to make sure there weren't any fires to put out with the housekeeping staff, then moved to the multitask printer to copy the threatening notes in the envelope. With both the originals and the copies back in her pocket she left her office to do a walk-through of the hotel before heading back to Antoine's suite.

The bulk of her work occurred in the mornings when she coordinated the staff to make sure all the rooms were cleaned and the guests' needs were met. She was not only responsible for the cleaning staff, but also for inventory of housekeeping items needed for the cleaning and maintaining of the guests rooms.

It was her routine in the evenings to walk through the hotel and be accommodating to any guest who might have a problem or simply to be a friendly face to both returning regular guests and new people who had come to enjoy the luxury resort.

She knew how important it was to offer a personal touch to the people who vacationed or came here for work purposes. She liked to think that her work here was at least part of the reason people chose to come back again and again.

When it was finally time to return to Antoine's suite a new tension began to well up in her stomach. The man definitely made her just a little breathless and she didn't like it. She didn't like it at all.

The last man who had left her breathless had not just broken her heart, but had shattered it into a million pieces. She'd never allow herself to be that vulnerable again. And she'd be a complete fool to entertain any feelings for a visiting prince who would soon return to his own life in his own country.

He'd obviously been waiting for her as he answered the door almost before her knock sounded. She stepped into the room and he closed the door behind her. "I made two copies of the notes," she said. "One for you and one for me." She handed him both the original and his copy.

"Why would you want a copy?" he asked curiously.

"In case something happens to yours," she replied and tried to ignore how her heart stuttered at his nearness. At five feet nine inches, Beth was unaccustomed to men towering over her, but Antoine was a good four or five inches taller. He made her feel small and feminine.

"If you'll get your driver, I'll give him directions to the forensic lab where we can find Jane," she said.

"You're going to be my driver," he replied smoothly. "I don't want anyone to know what we're doing, what we've found and that includes my entire security team. We must figure out a way to get me out of the hotel and to your car with nobody seeing me."

Beth stared at him, not only nervous at the idea of being alone with him but also by the fact that she would be responsible for him while he was with her. "But what if something happens? What if you get hurt?"

His sensual lips curved up in a smile that warmed the ice-blue of his eyes. "Unless you're planning on beating or maiming me, I should be just fine."

"But surely you should take somebody from your security team with you," she protested. She'd feel so much better if there was somebody big and burly and fully loaded with an arsenal of weapons.

The blue of his eyes paled to an icy silver and his lips thinned. "No. We go alone." His voice was laced with command and for the first time he looked and sounded like a prince accustomed to getting his way.

She frowned thoughtfully. "Okay, if you go down this hall to the end, there's another corridor, turn right and follow it and you'll

see an exit door. If you give me five minutes
I can pull up outside the door."

"Perfect, then I'll see you in a few minutes."

As Beth left the suite and headed back
to the lobby nervous anxiety pressed tight
against her chest. God forbid she had a
wreck while driving the Prince of Barajas.
Once again she found herself wondering
when exactly she'd lost her mind and when
she could hope for its return.

When she got into her car she quickly
scanned the interior, noting the tear in the
passenger seat, the faint layer of dust that
covered the dashboard. Not exactly fit for
royalty, but the ten-year-old car was paid off
and still ran perfectly well. He'd just have to
deal with the less-than-royal transportation.

She told herself that one of the reasons
she wanted to help him was because this
whole ordeal had hammered the hotel with
negative publicity. But she suspected the
truth of the matter was that she was desperate for something, anything that might fill

the vast loneliness in her life, even if it was just for a single night.

She pulled up against the curb by the door she'd told Antoine to exit and watched as he strode toward her. Once again she was struck by his handsomeness and as he flashed a quick smile to her a crazy burst of heat momentarily usurped her nervous anxiety.

"Mission accomplished," he said as he slid into the passenger seat. "Nobody saw my escape."

"Won't somebody worry if you aren't in your room?" she asked as she pulled away from the curb.

"I have my cell phone with me and told my staff that I was retiring for the night and didn't want to be disturbed for any reason. Nobody will even know that I'm missing from my suite," he assured her.

Beth gripped the steering wheel tightly and headed toward the small town of Dumont. The scenery was spectacular with the last gasp of the sun sparking off the distant mountains and painting the landscape in lush shades of deep gold.

Antoine looked out the window and even though he was silent she felt a pulsing energy radiating from him. He turned to look at her, as if he'd felt her surreptitious gaze. "Do you think Jane will help us?"

"If anyone can pull a print from those papers, she can," Beth replied. "But, she's a by-the-book kind of woman. She might insist that the notes be handed over immediately to Sheriff Wolf."

"Then I'll just have to convince her that that's not in our best interest," he replied with an easy confidence.

"She's pretty tough," Beth warned.

"Yes, but I'm pretty charming," he countered.

Beth gave a rueful laugh. "You charmed that envelope right out of my pocket."

He sobered and she felt his gaze, intense and piercing on her. "I had a feeling you'd found something important and it was equally important that I convince you to tell me."

"Do you always get what you want?" she asked lightly.

"It's certainly rare that anyone tells me no."

"I would imagine that being surrounded by yes-men could get a little boring at times."

"Perhaps," he replied and then cast his gaze out the side window once again.

The town of Dumont, Wyoming, was a small, charming place with historic buildings that dated back to the early 1800s. It had been a town filled with good, hardworking people before the royals had arrived. Now the streets were clogged with news vans and strangers.

Beth drove down the main drag and parked in front of the brick courthouse. "Jane's lab and offices are on the second floor," she said as she turned off the engine.

Antoine glanced at his wristwatch. "Won't the offices be closed by now?"

"Security will let her know we're here and it's rare that Jane isn't at work this late in the evening," Beth explained.

Together they got out of the car and she noticed that Antoine did a quick sweep of the area with his narrowed gaze. Apparently he saw nothing to cause him alarm and they walked to the front door of the courthouse where Beth gestured to the security guard inside.

Within minutes they were in the elevator taking them to the second floor and Jane. She met them at the doorway of her office, her hazel eyes widening as she saw Antoine. "Prince Antoine, Beth…what's going on?"

Antoine glanced up and down the hallway and then gestured to her office. "Ms. Cameron, perhaps we could speak to you in private."

"Of course." Jane ushered them into the small office and closed the door behind them.

"I was instructed today to pack up Sheik Amir Khalid's items in his suite to be stored until we know what happened to him or somebody from his family came to claim them. While checking the nightstand drawers I found an envelope taped to the bottom of one," Beth said.

Jane's eyes filled with interest as Antoine held up the envelope but didn't offer to hand it to her. "We'd like to see if you can pull some fingerprints from either the envelope or the notes inside, but before I give this to you I would like you to promise to keep this strictly confidential between the three of us."

Jane frowned and raked a hand through her curly light brown hair. "I can't make that promise without seeing what you have." There was a hint of steel in her voice.

Antoine held her gaze for a long moment and then offered her the envelope. "What I'm hoping is that you can lift some prints and then give us a little time to do some investigating on our own before letting anyone else know about it."

Jane didn't take the envelope from him, but instead opened her office door and gestured them outside. "Bring it into the lab. I don't want to touch it without gloves. As it is I'll need to print both you and Beth so we can discount your prints on everything."

They entered a small lab where Jane grabbed a kit from one of the metal shelves against the wall and then stepped up to a work table and pulled on latex gloves. Only then did she take the envelope from Antoine.

As she read the notes her eyes widened once again and when she finished she stared at first Antoine, then at Beth.

"These need to go to Jake," she said.

"Eventually I'll hand them over to him," Antoine replied. "But let's be serious here. The local law officials haven't exactly proven themselves to be good, upstanding people. Even your own boss was proven to be untrustworthy."

Jane's face flushed and she looked down at the notes she'd spread out on the table. Amos Andrews, Jane's boss, had not only tried to screw up her investigation into the bombing of the limo, he'd also tried to kill Jane. When he'd been arrested he'd made it clear that he was just a bit player in a larger

conspiracy against the visiting royals, hired
by somebody he refused to name.

"So, what exactly is it you want from
me?" she asked with a weary sigh.

"Just a little time," Antoine replied.

"How much time?" she asked.

"Seventy-two hours," he replied after a
moment of hesitation.

Jane said nothing. She opened the kit
and withdrew several brushes and powder
compounds in small bottles. As she began
her work, Beth couldn't help but gaze at
Antoine again and again.

He stood rigid and once again she felt
the energy wafting from him. And why
wouldn't he be tense? The stakes couldn't
be higher. Somebody wanted him and the
other participants in the COIN coalition
dead.

They didn't know at this time if the
people who were behind the conspiracy had
already achieved the goal of killing one of
them—Amir.

Antoine slid a glance at her and offered
her a small smile that shot a hint of warmth

in his cool blue eyes. Beth had always believed the term bedroom eyes meant dark
and smoky and slightly mysterious, but she
now recognized that bedroom eyes could be
the cool blue of a mountain lake.

"I hope you find a useable fingerprint,"
he said, his focus back on Jane. "When I
know the identity of the person who wrote
those notes, I will make certain he's never
a threat to anyone again."

His tone was light and easy, but with a
chilling undertone. Yes, he might make a
delicious lover, but she had a feeling he'd
make an even more formidable enemy.

IT WAS ALMOST NINE when they finally left
the lab after being printed by Jane. She'd
managed to pull another print that didn't
belong to either him or Beth and hoped that
whoever had left it behind was in the Auto-
mated Fingerprint Identification System. If
they were lucky she would have a name for
them sometime the next day.

"I'm too wound up to go back to the suite
and sleep." He turned to look at the woman

driving the car. He'd been acutely aware of Beth even as he'd tried to focus on what Jane had been doing.

He knew that to be successful in her position she had to be a strong taskmaster. The resort was known for impeccable guest services and housekeeping. And yet he sensed a softness in Beth that drew the darkness that resided inside him.

And there was darkness.

She cast him a quick glance and then returned her gaze to the road. "I'm a little wired myself," she admitted.

"Perhaps we could go back to your place, have a cup of coffee and talk about things."

He could tell he'd shocked her. "Prince Antoine, my home is small and simple. It's not exactly fit for a prince," she replied.

"A comfortable chair, some hot coffee and a little company is all I'd like. And please, call me Antoine."

"Then you can call me Beth. Coffee sounds good and then I'll be glad to take you back to the resort. My place is only ten minutes from there."

"Then it's settled, coffee at your house." He leaned back against the seat and stared out the side window into the darkness. *You're a cliché,* he thought ruefully. He was a prince who was afraid to trust anyone, with an aching depth of loneliness inside him and the mantle of power weighing heavily, definitely a cliché.

For the past three weeks Antoine had done nothing but worry and wonder about the attack, about what danger might come from what unexpected source.

He'd had long dialogues with the other men in the COIN coalition. Prince Stefan Lutece, Sheik Efraim Aziz, Sheik Amir Khalid and Antoine and his brother had all come here in the hopes of trade agreements with the United States that would benefit their small countries and instead had found nothing but treachery, danger and betrayal.

At the moment Antoine was sick of it all. The resort had become a place of intense stress, of people yammering at him and palpable tension that filled the air the moment he stepped out of his rooms. He was looking forward to a little more time away from the luxurious surroundings.

Beth turned off the road they had been traveling and onto a narrower road with deep embankments and thick trees on either side. "You drive this every night after dark?" he asked.

"It's the only way for me to get home. It's not too bad as long as you make sure you stay on the road."

A small laugh escaped him. "That would be an understatement. I'm sure it gets quite dangerous in the winter."

"I call this car my little engine that could." She tapped the steering wheel with a long slender finger. "Although I have to admit more than once in the winters somebody from the hotel has had to come to get me because I don't have four-wheel drive."

He could tell she was beginning to relax with each minute they spent together. He wanted that. For just a little while he wanted to be treated like an ordinary man and not like a prince.

"This feels very isolated," he said as the

trees on either side of the road seemed to crawl closer.

"It is. It's a pretty big spread but most of it hasn't been cleared or anything. My grandfather bought the land years ago, long before there was a resort. My father and mother chose to make it their home after my grandparents died and I've always lived here. I like the isolation, the beautiful nature that surrounds me when I step outside my front or back door. Is your country beautiful?"

"White beaches, blue seas, lush flowers… yes, Barajas is very beautiful, but I find Wyoming to be as beautiful, just different."

She turned off the road and onto a driveway that led to a small cottage. A light shone from the front porch, a welcome beacon in the darkness that had fallen. Colorful flowers spilled from boxes under the windows. It looked like something from a fairy tale, an enchanted cottage in the middle of the wilderness.

"It's not much," she said with a touch of defensiveness. "But it's all mine and I love it here." This time her words held an obvious sense of pride.

The sense of welcome that the porch light had emitted continued on into the house. As Antoine stepped inside the living room the earthy burnt orange and browns of the décor instantly put him at rest.

"Please, have a seat." She gestured him toward the overstuffed sofa. "I'm just going to get out of my uniform. I'll be right back to start the coffee."

She disappeared down the hallway and Antoine sank into the comfortable couch cushion and gazed around the room. Like subtle facial features that could give away internal emotions and weaknesses, he knew a room could speak volumes about the person who lived in it.

A bookcase stood against one wall, one of the shelves filled with framed photos of Beth with an older woman who appeared to be her mother. The television was small, as if watching it wasn't a top priority. A paperback lay on the end of the coffee table, the couple's clinch on the cover letting him know it was a romance novel. A wind chime tinkled a lovely melody from someplace outside the windows.

A lonely romantic who loved nature, he thought. There was no sign of a man's presence anywhere in the room. An old record player sat next to a stack of ancient LPs and it was easy for him to imagine her curled on the sofa with a book in hand while old, romantic music filled the house.

He looked up as she returned to the room, clad in a pair of jeans that looked slightly worn and hugged her long slender legs to perfection. Her mint-green T-shirt fit a little big but not so much that he didn't notice the press of her full breasts against the material.

He suddenly wished he was in a pair of jeans, on the back of a horse with her, her arms wrapped tightly around him as they rode carefree across a pasture. It was a vision that brought the first burst of pleasure he'd felt since arriving in Wyoming.

"Let's go into the kitchen and I'll make the coffee," she said.

He followed after her, unable to avoid noticing the way her jeans cupped her shapely buttocks. Why was there no man in her life? A woman like her should have a man to thrill her with his lovemaking and then hold her tight through the darkness of the night.

The kitchen was a surprise. Large and airy, with a breakfast nook that was surrounded on three sides by floor-to-ceiling windows, it was obviously the heart of the house. Gourmet copper-bottomed pans hung from a rack above the stove and a variety of cooking-aid machines lined the counters.

"You like to cook." He stated the obvious.

She flashed him a bright smile that warmed him in places he hadn't realized were cold. "I love to cook. It's my secret passion." She pointed him to the round oak table in the nook. "Have a seat. The coffee will be ready in just a minute and I have some leftover red velvet cake to go with it."

He sat and enjoyed the view of her bustling to get the coffee brewing. It had been far too long since he'd enjoyed the pleasure of a woman. For weeks before the trip to the resort there had been meeting after meeting to decide what to offer and what they needed from the trade agreements they intended to make. There had been almost no time for any kind of a social life.

"Hopefully Jane will have something for you tomorrow," she said as she placed a creamer and sugar bowl on the table. Then went back to the counter and returned with a platter holding a cake that looked as if it had just come out of a bakery.

"Hopefully," he replied. "But I don't want to talk about any of that tonight. Tonight I want to talk about ordinary things, things that don't set off a burn of anger in my belly. I noticed that you have a lot of pictures of you and your mother in the living room."

"Yes. My dad died when I was six and when I was thirteen my mom developed a severe heart condition. Unfortunately she passed away three years ago."

"My parents died when I was young." A long-remembered grief touched Antoine's heart. He thought about the horrific night of his parents' deaths often, recognized and never forgot the lesson he'd learned that night.

"I'm so sorry." She poured the coffee and carried the cups to the table, then sank down in the chair opposite his. "Was it some kind of an accident?"

"Actually, they were murdered." She gasped and he continued, "My father was initially my mother's bodyguard. He was an American, an ex-mercenary and they fell in love and married. Unfortunately my father had made many enemies in his past and that night those enemies found him and my mother."

"So, who raised you and your brother?"

"My mother's father, King Omar Zubira." A whisper of a smile curved his lips as he thought of the stern but loving man who had raised them. "He didn't approve of my mother's marriage and never really accepted my father, but he was a loving man to me and Sebastian, although I must admit we sometimes gave him a hard time."

"The twin thing?"

He grinned. "But, of course. Being an

identical twin can be quite amusing and Sebastian and I definitely used it to our advantage whenever possible. After grandfather died I was grateful to have Sebastian by my side to share the responsibility of ruling Barajas."

"It must be a huge responsibility, to run a nation," she said as she sliced the cake and shoved a generous piece toward him.

"Probably no bigger than running the housekeeping staff at a luxury resort," he replied. "To be truthful Sebastian carries much of the weight. He's a good man with a knack for politics and he'd do fine without me. But enough about me. What I really want to know is why you don't have a man in your life. Surely you meet men during the course of your work."

He picked up his fork and took a bite of the cake and noticed that her features tightened slightly and a whisper of hurt filled her eyes. It was there only a moment and then gone, but it let him know that at some time in the not so distant past a man had hurt her...hurt her badly.

"I don't date hotel guests and besides, I stay busy with my work and I'm not particularly interested in a relationship right now."

It was a lie, he could see the deception in her features. "That's a shame, because you have lips meant for kissing."

Her cheeks flushed with a becoming color. "And you're rather impertinent for a prince."

He grinned, enchanted by her. "The last woman who called me impertinent was my mother. I was seven at the time. Now, tell me about your mother."

As Beth related moments from her past with her mother, Antoine recognized that Beth was not only beautiful, but loyal to those she loved.

She told him about having to forgo college to help support herself and her mother, but there was no complaint in her voice, merely a stating of facts.

He liked that about her. He had no patience for whiners. He and Sebastian hadn't been allowed to whine after the murder of his parents.

"So, what did you do before you became one of the rulers of Barajas?" she asked.

"I was a military man." He raised his coffee cup to take a drink, hoping a sip of coffee would wash away the sour taste that always sprang to his mouth when he thought of the things he'd done for the sake of his country.

"And you? When you were young did you dream of being a ballerina? Or perhaps a princess?" he asked.

She laughed. It was a pleasant sound that wrapped around his heart and momentarily held him captive. "Not at all. I have two left feet and I always wanted to raise horses so I dreamed of wearing chaps and a vest rather than a princess's tiara."

He had a sudden vision of her naked except for her long legs encased in a pair of leather chaps and her full breasts spilling out of a tiny vest. Hot blood welled in the pit of his stomach, spreading warmth directly to his groin.

He shifted uncomfortably against the wooden chair and reminded himself that he was here with her because he wanted to use her knowledge of the locals to further his investigation, not because he wanted to take her to bed and teach her everything he knew about sexual pleasure.

"You know horses?" he asked.

"I started riding at the resort stables when I was little and worked the stables until I got the job in housekeeping," she explained.

"You have enough land to raise horses. Why haven't you already done it?"

"It took me until six months ago to pay off the last of the medical bills that my mother had accrued. I'm hoping to realize my horse dream in about five years. It's almost midnight," she said with a glance at the clock on the wall. "I should get you back to the resort. I have to be back at work around six-thirty in the morning."

He leaned back in the chair and smiled. "I've already made up my mind. I'll stay here with you for the night."

Chapter Three

Beth stared at him in horror. The idea of this man, this prince, sleeping beneath her roof horrified her. As it was, the whole afternoon and evening had taken on the surreal aspect of some kind of weird dream.

"I don't want you traveling back and forth from the resort this late at night alone," he said. "The road that leads here is too narrow, too dangerous to drive in the darkness."

A nerve throbbed in the side of her neck, a nerve that always acted up when she felt anxious. "But the spare bedroom doesn't even have a bed in it. I've been using it as a home office."

"The sofa looked nice and comfortable. All I need is a pillow and blanket and I'll be fine. I'll call Sheik Efraim and let him know I'm with you in case a problem arises." He pushed back his chair and stood as if the matter had been decided.

It was a half an hour later when Beth closed the door to her bedroom and sat on the edge of her bed. What a night. She still couldn't believe that a prince was now on her sofa sleeping beneath one of the patch-work quilts her mother had made years ago.

She changed into her nightshirt and went into the adjoining bathroom to wash her face before going to bed. Initially when the royals had first arrived at the hotel all she'd been focused on was the extra work their presence might make for her staff. She hadn't really thought about them as being men, just ordinary men with the weight of power on their shoulders.

And now she couldn't stop thinking about Antoine being a man—a very hot, take-your-breath-away kind of man. But even though he looked at her with a bit of hunger in his eyes, she wasn't about to fall prey to ridiculous fantasies about life with Antoine or any other man.

She certainly wasn't about to become an American dalliance for him. She could just see the headlines—The Prince and the Chambermaid. She couldn't help the small giggle that escaped her at the very idea.

Her feet were firmly planted in reality, had been since she'd been young. With her mother's illness there had been little time for fantasies.

There had only been one time when she'd allowed herself to fall into a romantic fantasy and the result had been an ugly mess.

There was no way she intended to fall into Antoine's bedroom eyes. He was here only until he solved the mystery of his friend Amir's disappearance from the bomb site. Once he'd accomplished his goals here he'd be gone.

She got into bed and as always fought against a well of loneliness that had been with her for the past year. She was twenty-nine years old, longed for love and a family, but the next time around she intended to be smart, to be wary. She'd make sure the man she gave her heart to deserved the gift.

She'd expected to have trouble falling asleep, but the moment her head touched the pillow sleep claimed her. She was instantly plunged into an erotic dream.

She was naked and clinging to Antoine's broad dark shoulders as his mouth made love to hers. His kiss held a mastery she'd never experienced, a silent command that she respond with every fiber of her being. And she did. It was impossible not to.

His strong hands stroked up the length of her bare back and then around to cup her breasts. Sweet sensations cascaded through her at his touch. She was on fire with her need for him. It didn't matter that he would be gone before she knew it, she only knew that she wanted what he offered, longed to stay in his arms.

A moan filled her head, not her own but rather his and not from her dream and not one of pleasure.

A louder, more tortured moan pulled her from her dream. Her eyes snapped open and for a moment she couldn't discern dream from reality.

Her heart pounded with a quickened rhythm as she sat up and shoved strands of hair away from her face. A glance at the illuminated clock next to her bed told her it was just after two.

The noise came again, this time louder, deeper and definitely not from her dream, but rather coming from someplace outside her bedroom door.

The prince!

Was he in trouble? Had somebody found out he was here and was now trying to strangle him or hurt him in some way? Oh, God, she knew having him here had all been a mistake!

She jumped out of bed and grabbed a flower vase from the top of the dresser, the only thing she could think of that might be used as a weapon, and then ran into the living room.

In the spill of the moonlight through the windows she instantly saw that there was no danger, that Antoine was not being strangled or beaten by an intruder. Rather he was obviously in the throes of a terrible nightmare.

She set the vase down at her feet and then crept closer to the sofa, trying not to notice how his powerful bare chest gleamed in the moonlight as he tossed and turned and emitted deep, mournful groans.

"Antoine," she whispered softly.

He groaned again, the intensity of it filling Beth with immense empathy. What sort of dreams could evoke the sounds of such pain, such an emotional outburst while sleeping?

She called his name again, this time louder, but it wasn't enough to pull him from his tortured sleep.

She stepped even closer to the sofa and lightly touched his shoulder—and found herself shoved against the wall, Antoine's hands wrapped around her neck as his eyes blazed with an unfocused fire.

He'd moved off the sofa in the blink of an eye. She would have screamed, but she couldn't. It had all happened so fast. Shock and the pressure of his hands against her throat kept her mute. For just an instant she wondered if he was going to kill her before he came fully awake.

Reaching up, she managed to touch his cheek and in that instant saw the flames in his eyes douse as a searing focus took their place.

He released a ragged gasp and dropped his hands to his sides. "Beth. Beth, I'm so sorry." He pulled her off the wall and wrapped her in his arms. His bare skin was warm and she burrowed into him as the shock of the moment slowly faded away.

"I might have killed you," he breathed into her hair as he tightened his arms around her.

She closed her eyes, delighting in the moment of being in his embrace. This wasn't a man who had gone soft with good living. He was all hard, lean muscle against her. "You should come with a warning label—dangerous when awakened," she murmured against his chest.

His hands smoothed down her back. "Why did you awaken me?"

She raised her head to look up at him. "You were moaning as if you were in terrible pain. It was obvious you were having a bad dream. I…I just wanted to get you out of your nightmare."

"It *was* a very bad dream." He reached up his hands and cupped her face. "Thank you for waking me and I'm sorry if I hurt you."

Before she could guess his next move, he'd made it, taking her mouth with his in a kiss that ripped her breath right out of her chest.

His lips plied hers with heat and even though in the back of her head she knew she should step away, stop the madness, she didn't. Instead she opened her mouth to him, allowing him to deepen the kiss by delving his tongue to battle with hers.

The fevered heat of his soft lips and the feathery touch of his tongue shot a well of want through Beth. His hands tangled in her hair as he pressed so close to her she could feel that he was aroused.

Instantly she knew this was a bad place to be—the middle of the night, a handsome prince holding her tight and a heart she didn't want broken again.

She stopped the kiss and moved out of his arms. "That probably wasn't a good idea." She was surprised by how breathless she sounded. "Hopefully you'll sleep okay now for the rest of the night," she said, her gaze not meeting his. "And now I'll just say good-night again."

She nearly ran back to the bedroom, grateful that he didn't try to halt her escape. Sinking down on the edge of her bed she tried to forget the taste of him, the feel of his warm body against her own.

He was sweet temptation, but she couldn't allow herself to get caught up in any kind of an intimate relationship with him. That was heartache just waiting to happen and she'd already been there, done that.

As she got back into bed she allowed her thoughts to go back in time, back to when she'd believed Mark Ferrer was the man who was going to be her happily-ever-after, when she'd believed that she was loved as deeply as she'd thought she had loved.

She'd learned a very important lesson from Mark—that men could take you into their arms, look you right in the eyes and lie to get what they wanted.

Beth didn't know how to have sex without meaning. She simply wasn't built that way. She wasn't capable of physical release without emotional connection.

Antoine's kiss had tasted of fevered passion, but she knew that's all he had to offer and that would never be enough for her. She finally fell asleep with the firm commitment to keep her distance from Antoine.

The next morning when she left her bedroom dressed in her uniform of the pencil-thin black skirt and the white blouse with a gold WRR on the breast pocket, Antoine was already up and dressed as well.

"Good morning," she said, hoping he didn't mention the kiss, praying for no awkward moments.

"Good morning to you," he replied. "I hope you don't mind that I took the liberty of using the shampoo in the bathroom when I showered."

"Not at all," she replied. "I don't usually cook breakfast, but if you want something before we leave I'd be glad to whip something up."

"That's not necessary. I can order something from room service when I get back to the hotel."

He seemed distant, antsy to leave, which was fine with her. Within minutes they were back at the hotel where she ushered him in through the employees' entrance so he wouldn't have to walk through the lobby.

"If Jane calls I can count on you to take me back to her?" he asked before they parted ways.

There was a part of her that wanted to back away from the whole thing, that needed to back away from him. The kiss they'd shared the night before had shaken her more than she wanted to admit.

But, there was a soft plea in his eyes

and she realized she was probably the only person he trusted at the moment and it was impossible for her to tell him no.

"Just let me know if you hear anything and we'll figure something out," she replied. She turned to head toward her office but paused as he softly called her name. She turned back to face him.

His eyes glittered with a flirting light that instantly created a pool of warmth inside her. "I look forward to kissing you again, Beth."

"Definitely impertinent," she replied and then turned on her heels and quickly walked away to the sound of his amused laughter.

Once she was in her office the routine of the day quickly took over and the morning flew by. She checked the schedule and the time cards to make sure all her staff had arrived and by ten o'clock had left her office to do room spot checks.

She gave soft reprimands when necessary and praise when earned. She knew her staff respected her, but they also liked her as well.

Maybe Jane won't find anything, she thought at noon when she hadn't heard from Antoine. Maybe whoever had left that print on the papers wasn't in the AFIS system. Maybe last night was the end of their little partnership.

That would be good, she told herself as she returned to her office for a bite of lunch. He was far too charming, far too attractive and that kiss had dizzied her head and momentarily swept reason away. She was definitely better off keeping her distance from him.

Still, it was almost impossible for her to get him out of her mind. More than once she found herself staring unseeing out her window as her mind replayed the vision of his muscled bare chest in the moonlight. Her lips wouldn't easily forget the taste of his mouth against them. As crazy as it seemed, her body felt branded by the intimate contact with his.

It was just after two when her cell phone rang and Antoine's deep voice filled the line. "Jane called. She has a name. I'll be waiting for you by the back door."

He gave her no chance to reply, but instead immediately hung up.

AS ANTOINE WAITED FOR BETH he was filled with tense energy. He hadn't asked Jane to give him the name over the phone, didn't trust that somebody else might be listening in. He couldn't be sure if her phones at her lab were bugged.

He'd spoken briefly with his brother that morning. Sebastian had sounded happier than Antoine had ever heard him and he knew it was because his brother had found love with a woman he'd helped protect against her ex-husband. She was the same woman who had witnessed Amir crawling out of the wreckage of the limo.

Jessica Peters had been reluctant to come forward since she and her little girl, Samantha, were in hiding from her ex-husband, a Russian by the name of Evgany Surinka. Eventually she'd come forward and her ex had found her. Sebastian had been forced to kill him and in the whole process he and Jessica had found love.

Love.

It was something Antoine would never allow for himself and he wasn't sure how Sebastian had managed to forget that enemies sometimes hurt the innocent people in one's life.

Antoine had made many enemies in his position as top interrogator for the military, enemies who would love to get to him by killing anyone he loved.

Antoine was determined not to make the same mistakes his father had made. He would never allow anyone to get close enough to him to be used as a target for revenge. He would never forget that his father had been unable to protect his mother from the men who had been seeking revenge.

That's what Antoine had been dreaming about the night before, when Beth had awakened him. In his nightmare he and Sebastian had been children and had been hiding as angry men had killed his parents.

His thoughts slid from his dream to that

moment when he'd held Beth in his arms. She'd been soft and warm against him, the thin material of her nightshirt barely a barrier between them. It had been a mistake to kiss her and it was a mistake he wouldn't mind repeating again and again.

Spending time with Jessica Peters's four-year-old daughter, Samantha, had shot a surprising desire inside Antoine, a desire for a woman to love and children to raise and a life much different than the one he'd led.

But, the choices he'd made for his country would forever keep him alone and with a loneliness deep in his soul that would never be assuaged.

As Beth's car pulled up against the curb he left the hotel and hurried toward her passenger door. He slid into the seat and instantly was enveloped by her floral scent.

"I hope I don't get you into trouble, taking you away from your work," he said.

She pulled away from the curb. "It's not a problem. The hotel manager is covering for me. I told him I needed to take some personal time off and since I rarely take any time off at all it was fine."

He nodded. "Good. The last thing I'd want would be to mess up your job, your life, before I return to Barajas." It was a reminder to himself not to get in too deep with her, not to think anymore about how sweet, how hot her kiss was and how very much he'd wanted to lose himself in her.

"I'm not about to let that happen," she replied firmly.

"You look tired."

"I am tired," she admitted. "I had trouble sleeping after I got back to bed." Her cheeks colored with just a hint of pink.

The kiss they'd shared had certainly made it difficult for him to go back to sleep. It had felt like it had taken hours for his body temperature to return to normal. "But your day has gone well so far?"

"A normal day. What about you?"

He tried to relax against the seat. "I spoke to my brother and also to Sheik Efraim."

"Did you tell them what we found?"

"No. I'm keeping this information to

myself for the time being and I would like to remind you to do the same."

She nodded. "The seventy-two hours Jane gave you is quickly ticking off," she reminded him.

"With a name from Jane I can hopefully find out what I need to help find Amir or at least know who might be behind those notes and the attacks." He turned to look at her. "You said you know the locals. What I'd like you to do for me is to make a list of anyone who has recently come to town, perhaps gotten a job at the hotel."

"We do pretty thorough background checks on all of our employees."

Antoine released a dry laugh. "Backgrounds can be hidden or made to look exemplary."

"I'll be glad to make you a list of the new hires," she replied as she pulled into the parking space in front of the courthouse. "And I'll make some subtle inquiries about new people who have come to town, but that's going to be a big task considering all the reporters who have camped out since you all arrived here."

"I think the person or persons behind these attacks would have arrived in town just before the reporters." He opened his car door, his stomach tight with nervous energy as he thought about the name Jane was about to give him.

Whoever had arranged for the limo explosion had also paid off local officials and henchmen. There was money behind this operation—lots of money.

If he could get a name, then maybe he could figure out exactly where that money was coming from instead of the idle speculation they'd all indulged in up until now.

All thoughts fled from his mind as they took the elevator to meet Jane. At the moment he was focused only on getting the name of the person who had handled those notes before him, the person who had sent them to Amir.

Why his friend hadn't shared the content of the notes with the others in the coalition was a mystery. There was no way of knowing exactly when Amir had received them, if he'd gotten them before he'd left his country or after he'd arrived in the States.

Had the person who had written them been the one who had picked up Amir at the bomb site? Was Amir now a prisoner or had he been killed and his body buried someplace out in the Wyoming wilderness that surrounded them?

Jane met them at the elevator door and ushered them into her private office. "I still don't feel right about not taking the notes to Jake," she said in greeting.

"You promised us some time," Antoine reminded her. "And from everything I've heard about you, you're a woman of your word."

Jane's cheeks flushed red and she lifted her chin. "And I'll keep my promise, but if you find out something you need to take all this to Jake, and if you don't, I will." Her voice was filled with steel, letting him know she meant business.

"You said you have a name for me."

Jane nodded. "Aleksei Verovick."

Antoine stared at her in stunned surprise. "Are you sure?"

"It was a perfect match," Jane replied.

"Do you know him?" Beth asked.

"I know of him. Verovick is reputed to be the second-hand man in the Russian mob," he replied, his mind racing with supposition. This was proof that the mob was behind the attacks on the royals. Or was it? It was also possible that Verovick had gone rogue. Certainly he was a man who would be capable of anything if the price was right.

"But why would the Russian mob care if you all made trade agreements with the United States?" Beth asked in confusion.

"They shouldn't care," he replied. "Unless somebody has bought them and is paying for them to care."

"Today is Tuesday," Jane said thoughtfully. "I'll give you until Friday evening and then I'm taking this information to Jake."

He could tell by the look on her face that there was no more wiggle room, that he wouldn't be able to talk her into any more time. "Then I'd better find some answers before Friday evening." He touched Beth's arm and gestured toward the door. "Thank you, Ms. Cameron. I appreciate your cooperation."

"You only have it for three days," she reminded him as he and Beth left the office.

"What are you going to do now?" Beth asked as they left the building and headed for her car.

"Do some research into Verovick and see if I can figure out who's paying him and his men to destroy the coalition, to destroy all of us. Do you have a computer at your place?"

"Yes. You want to do the research on my computer?" Her voice held a touch of surprise. "Your suite has a computer and Internet access."

"If you don't mind, I'd rather use yours. I don't know who might enter my room when I'm not there, who could access the history on my computer to see where I've been. I have to be careful."

"Then we'll go to my place," she agreed

easily. "You're welcome to use my laptop as long as you need to."

They got into the car and Beth started the engine. "I'm fairly ignorant about politics," she said as she backed out of the parking space. "I don't understand why anyone would want to stop what you all were doing here. A trade agreement between any of the COIN nations and the United States sounds like a win-win situation to me."

Despite the anxious burn in his belly, he smiled at her, unsurprised and charmed by her naïveté. "There are some people who believe that these trade agreements are just the first step of our nations being consumed by the United States. And then there are Americans who believe that we're all terrorists and this is just our way of attempting to infiltrate America's security."

"Small-minded bigots," she observed. "Not everyone from a different country is a potential terrorist and people who think that way are just ignorant."

He smiled at her again. "Too bad you aren't in charge of the world. I have a feeling if you were it would be a much nicer place."

She laughed. "I'm just in charge of laundry and cleaning supplies and that's enough for me, thank you very much."

Antoine shifted his gaze out the side window as she turned onto the narrow road that led to her cottage. "If it was somebody from the mob who picked up Amir the night of the bombing, then I can't think of any reason they would have of keeping him alive. I keep wondering if he's someplace out there, buried in the woods where nobody will ever find his body."

He was surprised by the sudden rush of emotion that welled up thick in the back of his throat.

Her hand, warm on his arm, pulled him back from where he teetered on the edge of grief. "You can't lose hope, Antoine. Until we know for sure, you have to keep hoping that he's still alive."

As she withdrew her hand from him, he smiled at her once again. "You're a good woman, Beth Taylor."

She smiled. "Not especially. I can be impatient with my staff at times." Her hands tightened on the steering wheel. "I lead with my heart and not with my head and that's caused me to make some bad decisions in the past."

"What sort of bad decisions?" he asked. He realized he wanted to know everything there was to know about her. She stirred a lusty passion inside him, but he was also curious about her as a person.

"It's not important right now," she replied and frowned as she gazed in her rearview mirror.

"Problem?" he asked.

"I don't know. There's a dark car coming up fast behind us. This road isn't meant for speed. I just hope he slows down before he tries to pass us on this narrow road."

He turned to look and saw the vehicle behind them approaching far too fast considering the road condition. "Surely he'll slow down," he said.

He turned back around and saw her eyes widen in disbelief. At the same time their car was smashed from behind with a force that snapped his head back.

Beth struggled to gain control of the car, but to no avail. Antoine felt the car go airborne and knew they were in deep trouble.

"Beth!" he cried as the world went topsy-turvy and then everything went black.

Chapter Four

Grinding noise and splintering glass. Beth's world was a place of chaos and pain as the sky became the ground and top became bottom.

The car seemed to roll forever before finally coming to rest upside down. Beth felt dazed and unable to make sense of anything. Her heart pounded so loudly in her ears she could hear nothing else.

The scent of gasoline and motor oil filled the air. Her arms hurt from trying to wrestle with the steering wheel and her ribs ached from the tight grip of the seat belt. Everything that had been on the floor of the car was now around her head, confusing her even more as she tried to make sense of what had just happened.

Someplace in the back of her mind where rational thought still existed, she realized she wasn't badly hurt. She wiggled her toes and flexed her fingers and realized it didn't appear that anything had been broken. She was lucky to be alive.

And then she remembered her passenger.

She snapped her gaze to him as she worked to unfasten her seat belt. His eyes were closed and blood oozed from an ugly gash on his forehead.

Her heart felt like it stopped beating in her chest. Was he dead? Oh God, had she killed the Prince of Barajas? She became aware of a discordant sound and realized it was her own sobs.

"Antoine," she cried as she finally managed to get herself free of her seat belt. She reached over and grabbed his arm and shook it.

"Antoine, please wake up. For God's sake you have to be okay." She couldn't bear it if he were dead. She gasped in relief as he issued a deep-throated moan and slowly opened his eyes.

For a moment they stared at each other and then he groaned again. "Beth, are you all right?" He seemed dazed as he looked around the car.

"Yes, I think so. What about you? Your forehead is bleeding."

"I'm okay. I was just knocked out for a minute." He drew a deep breath and the faint fog in his eyes began to clear. He worked on unfastening his seat belt. "I smell gasoline. We've got to get out of here."

Thankfully the front window had exploded outward, affording them an escape route from the wrecked vehicle. After some difficult maneuvering Antoine finally managed to go out the window first and then leaned back in to help Beth escape the car.

They staggered away from the hissing, steaming car and collapsed on the grass. Beth looked up to the road, unsurprised to find that the car that had hit them was no place to be seen.

For a moment she felt too stunned to think as she stared at the car that might have become their coffin. She looked back at Antoine who was swiping the blood off his forehead.

"We need help," she said. "Do you have your cell phone?"

He patted his pocket and grimaced. "It must have fallen out in the car when we tumbled."

"Mine's in my purse, someplace in the car."

"I'll get it," he said and started to rise.

"No," she exclaimed quickly. "You sit still. You've had a head bang. Besides, I'm smaller and can crawl back through the window easier."

She pulled herself up from the grass and had only taken one step toward the car when the sound of a gunshot cracked and Beth felt the whiz of a bullet come precariously close to her head.

Antoine reached up and grabbed her by the arm and slammed her down to the ground. She hit the earth with a thud and Antoine instantly covered her body with his.

Her brain short-circuited. What was going

on? Somebody had shot at her? She gasped as Antoine pulled a gun from an ankle holster she hadn't known he wore.

"Wha…what's going on?" she finally managed to sputter.

"Shh, be still." His features were taut as he gazed in the direction where the shot had come from. His eyes were narrowed and pale—and utterly dangerous-looking.

His muscles tensed and he seemed to be holding his breath. Another shot split the air, the dirt near them kicking up in a whirl of dust.

He muttered a curse beneath his breath. "We're vulnerable out here in the open. We've got to move." He scanned the area. "See the trees behind us?"

She craned her neck to see and then nodded. "Yes." Her voice sounded two octaves higher to her own ears. Terror squeezed her throat and roiled in her stomach, making her feel as if she might throw up at any moment.

"When I say go I want you to run for those trees. Run as fast as you can and don't look back." He slowly moved his body off of hers.

Fear screamed through her as every muscle in her body tensed with fight-or-flight adrenaline. She didn't want to run. She didn't want to move. She just wanted to go back an hour in time, when everything was okay.

"Get ready," he whispered. "Go!"

As she jumped up and ran for the cover of the trees he stood and began to fire his gun in the direction of the shooter while he followed close behind her.

Beth stopped when she reached one of the large trees. She wanted to hug the trunk that was now an obstacle for the shooter to get around. Antoine slid in beside her and wrapped an arm around her waist. "Okay?" he asked.

Hell no, she wasn't okay. Still, she nodded, too breathless to speak. She felt like she'd stepped out of a nightmare and straight into hell.

Antoine's cold, calculating eyes scanned the area once again. She wanted to ask him what he saw…who he saw, but she was afraid to speak in case the shooter might hear her.

"We need to stay on the move," he said softly. "We'll go deeper into the forest and work our way toward the resort. Be quiet and stay close to me."

Stay close to him? If she could, she would have glued herself to his chest. The trauma from the wreck had momentarily shot her into a bit of a fog, but the fog had completely lifted now and she was consumed by a terror she'd never felt before.

The only thing that made her feel slightly better was that he seemed cool and calm, so completely in control and not afraid at all. She didn't know if it was just an act and at the moment she didn't care. She only knew it made her feel a little bit better.

"We're going to run to those trees," he said and pointed to the left of where they stood. "Stay low and move fast. Let's go."

As they raced toward the next stand of trees, Beth expected a bullet to slam into one of them, but there was no answering gunfire.

"Maybe he's gone," she gasped as they once again reached cover.

"Or he's on the move to get closer to us," Antoine replied, his words doing little to assuage the jagged fear that ripped at her. "We need to keep moving. We don't want to be static targets."

They moved from cover to cover, pressing their bodies against trees and crouching in the brush. Each chirp of a bird overhead, any rustle of a small animal in the brush momentarily stopped Beth's heart.

After making half a dozen moves, she felt Antoine begin to relax a bit. His eyes weren't as pale as they had been and his features were less tense.

"I think maybe he's gone," he said. "If he was still around he would have popped off another shot or two by now. But we still need to stay on guard."

"Maybe he was afraid somebody heard the gunshots," she said hopefully. "It had to be somebody from the sedan. Our

wreck wasn't an accident. He intentionally rammed us from behind." Fear once
again raised a cold hand and gripped her
in a deathlike vise.

"Let's get back to the resort and then we
can figure it all out." He took her hand in
his and together they began to head in the
direction of the hotel.

Somebody had tried to kill them. First
with the car collision and then with a gun.
Had this been yet another attempt to kill
one of the men in the COIN coalition? Did
it have something to do with the notes they
had given to Jane?

There were so many questions and no
answers to make sense of what had just happened. All she knew was that she couldn't
wait to get back to the safety of the resort
and she didn't even want to think about the
fact that her car was now destroyed and the
insurance payment would be just shy of
paltry for the old reliable car.

They walked in silence for what felt like
hours. Every once in a while Antoine would
signal a stop and as they stood still he lis-

tened to the woods around them, his gun at the ready.

When the resort property finally came into view Beth almost wept in relief. Antoine looped an arm over her shoulder, as if to offer some comfort as they made their way to a side door that would keep them from having to enter through the lobby.

"We have to call the sheriff," she said as they entered his suite. "We can't keep this to ourselves. We have to report this, Antoine."

"You're absolutely right," he agreed and swiped at his forehead where blood still oozed from the gash. "But we don't have to tell him everything. We don't have to tell him that we were at Jane's or about the notes, just that we were on our way to your place."

She hesitated before replying. Lying was aberrant to Beth and she thought the time had come to tell Jake Wolf everything.

"Beth." Antoine placed his hands on her shoulders and gently kneaded with his fingers. "You've been so incredibly brave and I know this all has shaken you up, but I need you to help me. I need you to trust me enough to let me do what I need to do. I need the time that Jane promised us."

His eyes were soft pools of pleading and even though she knew she was probably all kinds of fool, she did trust him. "Okay, then we just tell him we were going to my house, that you wanted some time away from the resort," she finally relented.

"Thank you," he replied and dropped his arms back to his sides.

"I'll call Jake and then we need to clean up your forehead. You should probably be checked out by a doctor. If you were unconscious for any length of time then you probably have a concussion."

"Nonsense, I'm fine. No doctor." There was more than a little steel in his voice.

Minutes later, with the call made to Jake, Beth stood in the bathroom with Antoine. She tried to ignore his tantalizing nearness as she dabbed at his wounded forehead with a wet washcloth.

Even though they had survived a car crash and a shooter, despite the fact that they'd trekked through the woods to get back here, he still smelled of that wonderful cologne that danced delight in her brain.

"There's a lot of blood," she said, trying to stay focused on the task at hand. "You might need a stitch or two. I still think you should see a doctor."

"Head wounds always bleed a lot," he replied. "I'm sure it will be fine. I don't need a doctor." He was seated on the edge of the large tub, his face in a direct line with her breasts and she felt his gaze there, tightening her nipples beneath her blouse.

How could she be feeling so turned on after what they'd just been through? How could his nearness, his hand resting lightly on the small of her back, his simple gaze create such want inside her?

It had to be some sort of trick of adrenaline, she told herself. Hadn't she read something someplace about danger and sexual response? Something about endorphins or some hormone that made the two closely related?

"You have a soft touch." His deep voice

was like a warm caress as his breath fanned her collarbone.

"And thank God you have a hard head," she retorted.

He laughed and stood and she suddenly found herself in his embrace. "Nothing like escaping death to make you want to affirm life, right? And what I'd like to do at this very moment is carry you into my bed and make love to you until the sun comes up tomorrow morning."

Her breath hitched as she stared up at him. She knew that making love with Antoine would indelibly mark her forever, that when he returned to his country and his people, he would take a little piece of her heart with him.

But at the moment none of that mattered. What mattered was that his strong arms around her stole away the chill of residual danger from her. What mattered was that she couldn't remember ever wanting a man like she wanted Antoine.

When his mouth sought hers, she answered with a hungry kiss of her desire.

She tasted desire in his lips as well. His mouth demanded response and she gave, swirling her tongue with his as sweet sensations chased away the last of her fear.

She clung to him and wanted him to take her to his bed and make her moan with delight, gasp in sweet pleasure. She wanted to lose herself in him and not think about car crashes or crazy people chasing after them with guns.

His hands slowly slid down her back and cupped her buttocks and pulled her closer, tighter against him. He was aroused, but this time instead of pulling back from him, she wrapped her arms around his neck and pressed herself more intimately against his hard body.

"Sweet Beth," he whispered as his lips left hers and trailed a hot path down the length of her neck. "I want you." The simple words only increased her desire.

At that moment a knock fell on the door. Antoine groaned and with obvious reluctance released his hold on her. He stepped back, his eyes blazing with a hunger that threatened to devour her.

"This isn't finished," he said, his voice lower, deeper than usual. "I will have you in my bed, Beth Taylor."

The words were not a threat, but rather a promise that shot a shiver of anticipation up her spine as he turned on his heels and left the bathroom.

THE HEAT OF PASSION slowly ebbed as Antoine walked to the suite door. He'd expected Sheriff Jake Wolf, but instead he saw Michael, his head of security, on the other side of the door.

Michael gasped in alarm at the sight of him. "Your Highness, what happened? You've been hurt!"

"It's nothing," Antoine replied as he closed the door behind the big man. "I was in a car accident."

"A car accident? Why were you out in a car without your driver, without your security with you?" He didn't wait for Antoine to reply, but rather continued, "Your Highness, I can't keep you safe if you go off by yourself and don't let me know what's going on."

Michael's frustration was evident in his raised voice and the redness that filled his broad features. "These are dangerous times, Prince Antoine, and I take my job as head of your security team very seriously. I wish you would do the same."

"I'm sure Fahad Bahir, Sheik Efraim Aziz's head of security, took his job seriously as well," Antoine replied drily.

Michael sucked in a breath and froze. "You doubt my trustworthiness?" They both knew that Fahad had tried to kill Sheik Efraim but instead had been killed himself. "You wound me deeply. I would die to protect you," Michael exclaimed fervently. "You should know after all my years of service that your safety is my number one priority."

Suddenly Antoine was exhausted. The adrenaline that had pumped through him immediately following the crash, the raw, pulsing energy that had driven him through the woods to safety finally disappeared.

He sank down on the edge of the sofa as Beth returned to the room, looking as exhausted as he felt.

Michael raised a dark eyebrow at her appearance.

"Beth, this is Michael Napolis, head of my security team. Michael, Beth Taylor works here at the hotel as head of housekeeping." Beth nodded and slid down in the chair opposite the sofa as Antoine looked back at Michael. "We're waiting now for Sheriff Jake Wolf to arrive. We were forced off the road. We managed to escape the crash only to be shot at by an unknown person."

Michael's eyes narrowed. "I must insist that you use your security force whenever you leave these rooms. None of the members of the coalition who are still here are safe until we identify who is behind these attacks."

"We're safe for now. The sheriff is on his way and Ms. Taylor and I don't intend to leave this room for the remainder of the day. There are some things I want to go over with you later, but I'll call you when I'm ready."

It was an obvious dismissal and Michael knew it. He gave a quick bow and then left the suite. Antoine looked at Beth and for the first time noticed her clothes were dirty, her hose encasing her long legs were torn and she winced as she changed positions on the chair.

"You should go take a hot bath," he said. "You need to soak your muscles before they all tighten up. I have a clean robe hanging on the hook behind the door in the bathroom."

"Sounds like a plan," she replied but made no move to get up.

He stood and walked over to where she sat and held out his hand. "Come, it's been a difficult time and you look exhausted."

She took his hand in hers and allowed him to pull her up to her feet. "I'm more tired than I think I've ever been in my life," she admitted.

When they reached the bathroom, Antoine started the water running in the tub, added a liberal dose of scented bath salts and then walked back to her and gently cupped her face with his hands. "I'm so sorry about what happened."

She smiled, but it was obviously a forced gesture. "Don't you dare apologize. You aren't responsible for any of what happened. You didn't force my car off the road and you weren't the one taking potshots at us."

"I don't know what I would have done if you'd been hurt." Emotion welled up and pressed heavily in his chest as he thought of what might have happened to her. They'd been very lucky to walk away from not only the wrecked car, but also from whoever had been shooting at them.

"Thankfully the only real casualty was your head and my hose." This time her smile was more genuine, although still weary.

He held her gaze for another long moment, then let her go and stepped back. "Soak and relax. When Sheriff Wolf arrives I'll take care of the report to him. If he needs to speak to you I'll let you know." With that he closed the door to allow her privacy.

He would have loved to climb into the big tub with her, to feel her soap-slickened skin against his, but he had business to attend to and couldn't afford to allow himself to get distracted again by Beth's charms.

Although he'd been reluctant to use the computer in his room to do the search he wanted to run, he also didn't want to waste time. He needed to find out everything he could about Aleksei Verovick as soon as possible.

As he waited for the computer to power up he made a couple of phone calls, taking care of some business that needed to be handled and by that time Sheriff Jake Wolf arrived.

"Sheriff Wolf." Antoine ushered in the tall, Native American sheriff who had a reputation for being a straight shooter.

Despite his reputation, Antoine wasn't at all sure whether to trust the man. According to what Antoine had heard, there had been whispers of corruption in the Wind River County law enforcement for many years.

"Prince Antoine, when Beth called me she said you needed to report a crime," Jake said.

"Please, have a seat." Antoine gestured him toward one of the easy chairs next to the sofa.

"Where's Beth?"

"She's in the bathroom cleaning up." Antoine shoved aside a quick vision of Beth in a tub of bubbles. "We've had a rather traumatic afternoon. It started when a black sedan intentionally rammed us from behind and forced Beth's car off the road and down an embankment near her cabin."

Jake sat up straighter in his chair, his dark eyes glowing with intensity. "Did you get a plate number? Maybe see who was behind the wheel?"

"Unfortunately no." How Antoine wished he'd seen who had been driving that car. How he wished he'd gotten an eyeful of the person who had been shooting at them. If he had, they would now no longer be a threat.

"It all happened so fast. The car plowed into us, we went off the road and flipped a couple of times, but Beth and I managed to climb out of the wreckage. Thankfully we were both wearing our seat belts so sustained simply bumps and bruises."

"And a pretty good gash on your forehead," Jake observed. "Do you need to see a doctor?"

Antoine raised a hand to the wound which had finally stopped bleeding. "No, it's fine. Anyway, by the time we managed to climb out of Beth's car, the other car was gone, but somebody started shooting at us."

Jake released a weary sigh. "And I suppose you didn't get a look at who was doing the shooting."

"I'm afraid we were too busy scrambling for cover to pay much attention. Eventually the shooter must have left the area and we made our way back here."

"You had no security with you?" Jake

lowered his dark eyebrows in obvious disapproval.

"Beth and I were on our way to her place. I felt a need to escape everything and everyone, and that included my own security team."

Jake frowned. "You royals would make my life much easier if you'd either avail yourself of your own security or stay holed up here in your rooms. Better yet, perhaps it's time to wrap things up here and head back to your country."

"That's not going to happen until I find out about Amir's fate," Antoine replied firmly. "I understand the difficulties our being here has brought you and I apologize for that, but I have no plans to return to Barajas at the moment."

Jake waved a hand. "I guess it's all in a day's work," he replied. "At least I can't say things have been boring around here lately. So, let's start at the beginning and you tell me exactly what happened again."

It was almost an hour later that Jake left the suite with what little information

Antoine had been able to give him. Jake had made arrangements for Beth's car to be towed although Antoine was relatively certain it couldn't be salvaged for anything but junk.

The minute Jake left Antoine headed toward the master bathroom to check on Beth. She hadn't put in an appearance the entire time that Jake had been there.

He discovered the reason for her absence the minute he walked into the bedroom. Clad in his white robe, she was curled up asleep in the middle of his bed, a hand towel folded up and clutched in one hand. As he watched her sleeping he felt his heart constrict just a little bit.

During the entire trek back to the resort she hadn't complained. She hadn't worried about the fact that she now didn't have a car. She hadn't accused him of getting her into a bad situation. Her entire concern seemed to be getting him back to the resort so she could take care of the cut on his forehead.

She was unlike any woman he'd ever met before and she was definitely getting under his skin. She looked so beautiful with her long lashes dusting her cheeks and her lips slightly parted as if anticipating a lover's kiss.

Despite his words about taking her to bed, he knew the best thing he could do for both of them was to back away. When she woke up he needed to take her back to her cottage and then leave her alone.

The last thing he wanted was to bring danger to her doorstep and this afternoon had been too close a call for him to want to continue having her near him.

Antoine stared at her for a long moment. He'd never wanted to get too close to a woman because he'd never wanted to feel responsible for a woman's safety.

He'd never forgotten that his father's past had lunged up to destroy not only his own life, but Antoine's mother's life as well. Antoine was determined not to make the same mistakes as his father.

As quietly as he'd entered the room he left, more confused than ever about what to do with her.

They had gotten little sleep the night before and with the dramatic events of the day he knew the best thing for her at the moment was sleep. That would allow him to figure out whether he should cut her loose or keep her close.

He returned to his computer to find out what he could about Verovick. He didn't know how long he worked before darkness and hunger drove him back out of his chair.

He ordered dinner from room service and turned on lights against the night, then once again checked on Beth who was still sleeping soundly.

There was a part of him that wanted to get into the bed with her, to pull her warm sleeping form against him and allow himself to relax for the first time in hours.

However, Jane's clock ticked loudly in his head, reminding him that minutes were slipping by and he had only two days left before she'd take the information in the notes to Jake Wolf.

He returned to the desk and stacked the

pages he'd printed off the computer. He leaned back in the chair and began to read.

There was no question that plenty of speculation swirled around Aleksei Verovick with little solid fact. He was reputed to be behind a scam that had stolen hundreds of credit card numbers and personal information that had yielded hundreds of thousands of dollars for the mob.

His name had been linked to kidnappings and killings, but a lack of solid evidence and plenty of palm-greasing had apparently kept him a free and very powerful man.

He picked up one of the printouts and stared at a photo of the man. Verovick had a thick, beefy body and a square head with a prominent jaw. His hair was dark and cut with military precision and his eyes were round and black like those of a reptile. He looked like a formidable enemy to have.

Antoine frowned as he noticed the fountain in the background of the picture. It was large and made of stunning marble, with finely sculptured sea nymphs rising out of the huge base.

He knew that fountain, had stood before it many times when he'd visited the island of Saruk. In their area of the sea there were a total of five independent islands—Barajas, Kyros, Nadar, Jamala and Saruk.

Saruk was the largest of them all and the only one that had chosen not to participate in the COIN coalition.

So, why would a man like Aleksei Verovick be visiting in Saruk? More important, who had he been visiting while in that country? Antoine's mind raced with theories.

Kalil Ramat, the leader of Saruk, had made no secret of the fact that he disapproved of the COIN coalition and their goals, but surely his disapproval wouldn't go so far as to hire members of the Russian mob to destroy the leaders of the other nations.

Antoine picked up his phone and dialed his friend, Darek Ramat, Kalil's son.

"Antoine." Darek's deep voice held a warm welcome when he answered. "How are you, my friend?"

"Good," Antoine replied. He figured the fewer people who knew about the attacks against him and the others, the better.

"It's good to hear you're well."

"It's good to be well," Antoine replied with a touch of humor. "And how are things on the beautiful island of Saruk?"

"Wonderful. I have plans tonight to club it with a couple of beautiful women so life is definitely good," Darek said with a hardy laugh. "And when are you planning a visit here?"

"I don't know, Darek, things are still very much up in the air with nobody knowing anything about Amir."

"I pray for his safety," Darek replied. "There have been no new developments?"

"None," Antoine replied and felt the edge of grief he always suffered when thinking about Amir. "Aleksei Verovick, you know the name?" Antoine asked, getting to the point of the call.

"No, should I?" There was obvious confusion in Darek's voice.

"He's reputed to be a high-power player

in the Russian mob and he was recently a visitor to your country."

"Really? Well, I don't know the man. I have nothing to do with reputed mobsters."

"So you would have no idea what he was doing in your country?"

"Antoine, many people visit Saruk. This is a beautiful place where tourism thrives. Do you think this man has something to do with Amir's fate?"

"Perhaps," Antoine replied, not wanting to tell Darek about the notes that had been found, notes that were directly tied to Verovick.

The two men talked for a few minutes longer and then hung up. Antoine leaned back in his chair and fought against a new wave of exhaustion.

Was it possible that Kalil's disapproval had gone over the top? Had he taken his disapproval of the COIN coalition to the next level and actively worked against them by hiring the Russian mob to take them all out?

Antoine had a difficult time believing

that about a man who had many times opened his household to him in welcome, a man who was the father of somebody Antoine considered a good friend.

Had Verovick simply been vacationing on the beautiful island of Saruk? He supposed even mobsters needed a vacation now and then.

A knock on the door pulled him from his thoughts. Dinner had arrived. As the server left the suite Beth appeared in the doorway from the bedroom.

She had dressed back in her own clothes sans the ruined pantyhose and looked far more refreshed than he felt.

"Ah, sleeping beauty awakes. I hope you like steak," he said. "I took the liberty of ordering a late-night dinner for us."

"It smells delicious and right now I think I could eat anything you put in front of me." She walked across the room to the dining room table where the plates had been placed with meticulous care. "Did Jake come?"

He nodded. "He did. I made the report and Jake will be looking for a dark sedan with front-end damage. There's no way that car could have hit us with such force and not sustained some damage."

"I'm sorry I slept through it all. After the bath I sat on the edge of the bed and before I knew it I was out like a light."

"I had Michael pick up replacement cell phones for both of us," he said.

"Thanks."

She sat at the table. "And once we finish eating I'll call somebody on staff to take me back to my place."

"That won't be necessary," he replied. "I bought you a new Jeep, complete with four-wheel drive and all the extras. It's down in the parking lot now with a red ribbon tied to the antenna."

He'd expected joy to light her eyes, or at least a little bit of relief that she didn't have to worry about not having a vehicle anymore. He'd sent Michael to take care of the details and Michael had managed to get everything done while she'd slept.

But, instead of joy, her green eyes narrowed and her lips thinned with a hint of displeasure. "I didn't ask you to buy me a new car."

"No, you didn't," he replied easily. "That's not in your nature. But, you needed a new one and so I got you one."

"I can't accept a new car from you."

"Of course you can," he replied and sat next to her at the table. "It's already tagged and licensed in your name. It was because of me that your car was destroyed. Don't look at it as a gift, but merely a replacement of the one I ruined."

What he didn't tell her was that a tracking device had been placed on the Jeep to allow him to keep track of her movements by his computer. It was just a precaution, given what they'd just experienced.

Her cheeks were flushed pink as she stared at him. "I'll make payments to you until I've paid for it, every dime that it cost you."

Damn, but he wanted her now, this very minute with her eyes blazing and her chin thrust forward in a show of stubborn defiance. But, as much as he'd like to think of his own wants, his own needs, he couldn't forget what had happened to his mother and father.

It was time to let her go.

Chapter Five

Beth sat at her desk the next morning with a cup of coffee in hand and thought about the night before. They had been halfway through dinner when Antoine had told her he didn't feel comfortable with her going back to her cottage alone.

Truthfully, she hadn't felt all that good about going home alone, either. The small house was far too isolated for her to be comfortable there alone after what had happened to them.

Antoine had told her she was welcome to stay in his suite, but she knew where that would lead and she wasn't willing to go there with him.

Once she'd slept good sense had prevailed and the desire she'd felt for him while the two of them had been in the bathroom had ebbed.

The fact that in the blink of an eye he'd bought her a new car reminded her of how very different their worlds were, how foolish she would be to think that there was any kind of future with Prince Antoine Cavanaugh.

She'd wound up spending the night in a hotel room that was available for staff and she always kept a spare uniform in her office.

She'd spent the night tossing and turning, thinking about what had happened with the car wreck and the shooting and ultimately her thoughts had returned to Antoine.

She took a sip of coffee and rose from her chair, ignoring the faint groan of muscles that had been overworked in the accident. She stared out the window, unseeing, lost in her thoughts.

People who stayed at the hotel were in transition. They were coming from somewhere or going someplace. They were conducting business or on vacation and had lives that had nothing to do with their stay at the resort.

Other than Mark she had never allowed herself to get involved in anything personal with a guest, aware that this was just a short stop in their lives that had little to do with reality.

There had been plenty of men who had flirted with her, who had made it clear that they might have pursued her given half an opportunity, but she'd shut them down easily.

Still, she was precariously close to losing her heart to Antoine. Not only was he handsome as sin, as sexy as satin sheets, but he was also a kind man and had a great sense of humor. He'd even started her bathwater for her. Damn, he was absolutely killing her.

If the knock on the door hadn't stopped them, they would have fallen onto Antoine's bed and made love. She'd been ready to succumb to him, to give herself completely with no thought of tomorrow. It would have been foolish to do so.

"Beth?" Barbara Kintell, one of the maids,

stuck her head into the room. "Do you have a minute?"

"Of course," Beth replied, grateful to focus on work and not on the wondrous charms of Antoine Cavanaugh. This was where she belonged, dealing with hotel housekeeping business and not anywhere near a prince who had everything it took to break her heart.

It was noon when Beth realized she'd promised Antoine the night before to look at the personnel records and see who had been hired in the weeks before the royals had arrived.

It was possible somebody here at the hotel had seen Antoine and Beth leave together the day before and had been responsible for what had happened after they'd left the lab.

This thought brought with it a sense of personal betrayal. Beth had always considered the staff here at the resort part of her extended family. She didn't want to believe that anyone here could be guilty of such duplicity.

It was also possible somebody in town

had seen them together and had decided it was a perfect opportunity to take out another member of the COIN coalition.

Beth spent most of her waking hours here at the hotel and rarely went to town for anything but groceries or to meet a friend for dinner.

There was one person who would probably know any newcomers in town and that was Beth's friend, Haley Jenkins, who worked at the most popular café in Dumont.

She dialed Haley's number and smiled as her friend's voice filled the line. "Hey girl, I haven't heard from you for a while. I was beginning to think you'd fallen off the face of the earth."

"I've just been really busy here at work," Beth replied.

"Rubbing elbows with all those hunky sheiks, I'll bet," Haley said.

Beth laughed although she felt the warmth of a blush on her cheeks. "Actually, a prince rather than a sheik," she admitted.

Haley squealed in delight. "Do tell all!"

"There isn't a lot to tell," Beth said hurriedly. "I've just been spending a little time with Prince Antoine Cavanaugh, but it's strictly on a professional basis. I'm helping him with a little investigative work."

"Beth, I've seen photos of him and his twin brother. They are definitely the hottie twins. I hope some of your work is under-cover…as in under the covers of one of those big, king-size beds."

Beth laughed once again and tried not to think about her and Antoine under the sheets of his bed, making love. "Not hardly. The reason I called is because I'm trying to get the names of people who came to town just before the visiting royals arrived, people who seem to have no real reason to be here."

"God, girl, that's a tall order. With all the reporters and journalists and all those kooky protestors, it's hard to figure out who has a reason to be here and who doesn't."

"This would be somebody who isn't a journalist, somebody who is probably a loner," Beth replied.

"Can I give it some thought and get back to you?" Haley asked.

"Of course," Beth replied. "And Haley, I really appreciate it."

"Whatever I can do to help. But, I will tell you that sooner or later I'm going to want details about you and the handsome prince."

Beth laughed again and when she and Haley hung up she typed in the password on her computer that would take her to the personnel files.

It took an enormous staff to keep a hotel and resort of this size running smoothly and Beth intended to check new hires for any position on staff.

It took her most of the afternoon to plow through the records with interruptions to attend to normal housekeeping duties and coworkers popping in just to say hello.

There was very little turnover at the hotel. People who worked here liked what they did and knew that in this economy good jobs were hard to find. The hotel provided not only comfortable wages, but excellent benefits as well and there was definitely a certain prestige in working for the Wind River Ranch and Resort.

However, she did find one name, a member of her own staff, who had been hired a little over a month before the royals had come to the resort.

Janine Sahron had told Beth when she'd been hired that her husband was from a small Mediterranean island and that they had recently moved to Dumont. At the time the information had meant nothing to Beth, but now she had to wonder about it.

Was it possible they had moved to Dumont specifically to get Janine hired, specifically to infiltrate the hotel and gain access to knowledge about the movements of the members of the COIN Coalition?

Beth grabbed her cell phone and called Antoine. She tried to still the leap of her heart as he answered, his deep sexy voice washing over her in a wave of heat.

"Beth, I was just thinking about you," he said in a distinctly sensual tone.

She wanted to tell him to stop it, to stop thinking about her, and to stop saying her name as if he were making love to it. "I was just thinking about you, too. I have a name for you—a maid who was hired a month before you all arrived here. I also remember her telling me that her husband was from a small Mediterranean island."

"What's her name?" Antoine asked, all softness gone from his voice.

"Janine Sahron."

"Sahron," he repeated the name thoughtfully. "Doesn't sound familiar, but that doesn't mean anything. I would like to meet with her immediately. Can you arrange it for me?"

"Unfortunately today is her day off," Beth replied.

"You have her address?"

"Yes, but what are you planning to do?"

"You and I will pay her a visit at her home. I will interrogate her and her husband and get the truth from them."

A faint shiver walked up Beth's spine at the cool resolve in his voice. "Shouldn't you call them first and let them know you're coming?"

"Absolutely not. I would prefer the element of surprise. So, when are you available to take me to them?"

She had told herself that she was done with Antoine, that what she needed more than anything was to distance herself from him, but she also knew that he had nobody he trusted as much as her. And the truth be told, she didn't want to distance herself from him—at least not yet and at least not physically.

"I can take off at about six this evening," she finally said and tried to ignore the dance her heart did at the thought of seeing him again. It didn't mean they would sleep together, she reminded herself. Helping him and sleeping with him were two very different things.

With arrangements made for her to meet him at the side door, they hung up. Beth directed her gaze out the nearby window where she had a view of the stunning formal gardens.

Was it possible that Janine and her husband were somehow tied to the Russian mobster who had written those threatening notes? It was so difficult to imagine the red-haired, blue-eyed, soft-spoken Janine involved in any kind of international intrigue.

But she reminded herself that lately the news had been filled with stories about spies living like the Joneses next door, people who looked like Sunday-school teachers and Boy Scout leaders who were actually planted for years as deep-seated spies.

Who would have thought that some of the local law could be bought off, that professional security teams could be compromised? She couldn't imagine living a life where you didn't know who to trust, where even the people closest to you could betray you in the blink of an eye.

Was it any wonder that Antoine found it easier to trust a virtual stranger like her than anyone close to him?

By the time six o'clock arrived nervous energy coursed through her. She was determined to take Antoine where he needed to go, support him in what he had to do, and yet try to maintain a healthy emotional distance from him.

That emotional distance was difficult to maintain the minute she slid into the interior of the new black Jeep. Despite the fact that Antoine had been suffering from a gash in his forehead and from the trauma of somebody trying to kill him, within minutes of getting to safety he'd thought about her and the fact that she no longer had a car she could use.

Sitting in the new beige leather seat, smelling the new-car scent that surrounded her and staring at all the bells and whistles he'd included, she felt a wave of emotion press tight in her chest and bring a haze of tears to her eyes.

Nobody had ever done anything so nice for her before and while she intended to pay off every dime, she couldn't help but be touched that he'd thought about what she'd lost, that it had mattered to him.

She sucked up the uncharacteristic sentimental tears and headed for the side door where Antoine awaited. As always her pulse raced at the sight of him.

Although he wore his customary black dress slacks, this evening he had on a pale blue short-sleeved dress shirt that both showed off his biceps and emphasized the blueness of his eyes.

As he slid into the seat next to her and gave her the smile that threatened to turn her into a puddle, she knew maintaining any kind of emotional distance from this man was next to impossible.

Somehow he'd managed to dig in beneath the defenses she'd erected after the debacle with Mark. The lyrics to a Mariah Carey heartbreaker flew through her head, a reminder that she desperately had to quickly rebuild the defenses to keep her heart safe.

"You slept well last night?" he asked once they were headed in the direction of the Sahron residence.

"I would have slept better in my own bed, but yes, I slept okay. What about you?" She cast him a quick glance and noticed that he looked tired. The lines around his eyes appeared to cut deeper than they had the day before. "Nightmares?"

"No, no dreams. There were just too many thoughts in my head for me to sleep well," he replied.

"You need to talk about your thoughts?"

He cast her a warm smile. "I'm not used to sharing my thoughts with anyone, except perhaps Sebastian." He leaned back in the seat and a frown tugged his dark eyebrows downward. "I keep trying to figure out how to tie Aleksei Verovick to everything that has happened. I keep wondering if perhaps he's here in town and pulling strings behind the scenes."

"I called a friend of mine at a café in Dumont to see if she could give me a list of anyone who had come to town in the weeks before you all arrived. I haven't heard back from her yet. But sooner or later everyone who comes to Dumont eats at that café."

"You're a very smart woman, Beth."

She hated how she warmed at his words of praise. "If I don't hear back from her today, I'll give her a call first thing in the morning."

"I don't know what I would do without you, Beth. Without Sebastian here I have nobody else I can trust." She felt his gaze on her.

"Do you really worry that you can't trust your own security team?" she asked.

He frowned once again. "I want to trust them, but I'm naturally wary after what happened with Sheik Efraim's head of security. The promise of money and power can corrupt even the truest of heart."

"Money has never meant much of anything to me, except as a way to eventually finance my dream of owning horses," she replied. "I've never longed for designer clothes or fancy shoes. I love my simple life."

"A simple life sounds wonderfully attractive to me at the moment," he replied.

They both fell silent as she reached the Dumont city limits and she turned onto the street where the Sahron family lived.

"It should be just ahead," she said as she

slowed to read the numbers on the mail-boxes.

The Sahron house was a two-story that looked as if it was in desperate need of a face-lift. The white paint was peeling and weathered and some of the dark green shut-ters at the windows hung askance. The lawn was wild and dead bushes lined the side-walk.

"Apparently money is an issue with the Sahrons," Antoine said drily as she stopped the car in the driveway.

"I'll go up and knock on the door," Beth said. Although she was relatively certain they had not been followed and hopefully nobody knew about her new vehicle, she didn't want Antoine standing on the porch and potentially making an easy target for somebody.

"We'll go together," he replied firmly and opened his car door.

So much for attempting to save a prince, she thought as she got out. Although An-toine definitely wasn't the kind of man who would ever need saving by a woman. With his military training and his quick mind he could probably take care of himself in most situations.

She felt a nervous flutter in her stomach as Antoine rang the doorbell. She didn't want to think that a member of her own staff might be at least partially responsible for the horrible things that had befallen the visiting dignitaries.

Janine Sahron was a hard worker and a team player. She was a soft-spoken woman whom Beth had instantly liked. Was it possible Beth had completely misjudged her character? Janine had melded seamlessly into the team which was why Beth hadn't thought about her until she'd looked over the files.

It certainly wouldn't be the first time she'd misjudged somebody. A vision of Mark filled her head. Mark with his charming smile and laughing brown eyes. Oh yes, he'd fooled her with his promises of love and marriage and she'd bought into each and every one of his lies.

Her attention returned to Antoine as he

knocked on the door with an impatient rap. "I guess they aren't home," he finally said in frustration after knocking a second time.

"What now?" Beth asked as they returned to the car.

"I think we should park along the curb across the street and do what you call a stakeout."

"If that's what you want," Beth replied. "But, it's possible they're out for the evening."

Within minutes they were parked where he'd indicated with the engine off and the windows down to allow the refreshing evening air to flow around them.

"We'll give it an hour or so," he said. "And while we wait you can tell me about the man who broke your heart."

She looked at him in surprise and a small, uncomfortable laugh escaped her lips. "What makes you think some man broke my heart?"

His eyes gleamed a silvery blue in the waning light of day. "It's the only thing to explain why a woman like you is still alone."

She broke eye contact with him and stared unseeing out the front window as her mind drifted back in time. "I always had a firm policy not to date any of the guests who stayed at the hotel. It just seemed smart not to get involved with men who were there on business or on vacation and had lives to get back to."

"But, you made an exception," he said softly.

She turned back to look at him and nodded. "Yes, I did. His name was Mark Ferrer. He was some sort of a medical salesman who worked the state of Wyoming and about every two weeks or so he'd spend a couple of nights at the resort. I ran into him in town one evening. He had just finished up a business call and I was in town to buy some groceries. We bumped into each other and he invited me to have a drink with him."

She thought about that night. It had been the one-year anniversary of her mother's death and she'd been filled with an aching loneliness. "On impulse I decided to take him up on the invitation."

"And that was the beginning." It wasn't a question but rather a statement of fact.

"Yes, we started seeing each other whenever he was in town and he'd call me during the time he wasn't in town. He told me he lived in a small town about three hundred miles from here." Once again she cast her gaze out the window. "He was very romantic, seemed to be head over heels in love with me and it wasn't long before I believed I felt the same way."

She removed her hands from the steering wheel and felt the faint tick of the errant nerve in the side of her neck. It was embarrassing to admit how incredibly foolish she'd been.

Antoine reached over and took one of her hands in his. As always when she looked at him she wanted to fall into his arms, lose herself in the blue waters of his eyes. "You loved him and he didn't love you back?"

She wished it had been that easy. Unrequited love would have been a cakewalk compared to what she'd been through with Mark. "No, he professed to love me desperately up until the very end when I told him to get out of my life and stay out forever."

Antoine looked at her in confusion. "I don't understand. What happened?"

Beth sighed. "One night Mark stayed with me and the next morning when he left I realized he'd forgotten his briefcase. That evening I looked up his home number in the hotel records and I called him. To my surprise a woman answered the phone, a woman who introduced herself as Mark's wife."

How well she remembered that moment of shock, of utter betrayal that she'd felt. Married? Mark was married? Worse than that, she'd heard the sound of young children in the background.

She would never forget how humiliated she'd felt at that moment, how her heart had ached not only for herself but also for the woman on the other end of the line.

"What did you tell her?" Antoine asked.

"That I was head of housekeeping here at the hotel and Mr. Ferrer had left his briefcase in his room. She thanked me and told me Mark would be in touch."

"And I'll bet he was," Antoine said drily as he gently squeezed her hand.

"He called me an hour later, told me that nothing had changed between us. He said he loved me and was grateful that the truth was finally out. He said his wife didn't understand him, that she was jealous and vindictive but ultimately he didn't want to divorce her because he had to think about his children. He told me that now that the truth was out, there was really no reason why we couldn't keep the status quo."

The words tumbled out of her. She'd never shared this with anyone. Not even her best friends had known about Mark's ultimate betrayal.

"He assured me that nothing had changed between he and I, that he still loved me, still wanted to be with me whenever it was possible. I was appalled. I don't do affairs."

"Of course you don't. So, that was the end of it?"

She frowned. "For the next three months Mark called me incessantly. He couldn't believe that I didn't want to be with him anymore. He sent me flowers and candy and other gifts. I finally changed my cell phone number, but he'd call me at work."

"Did you think about filing a restraining order of some kind?"

"No. I didn't want to destroy his life. I didn't want his wife to know what he'd done. I just wanted him to leave me alone. Finally one day he stopped calling, stopped trying to make contact. That was almost a year ago. He hasn't been back to the hotel since and I figure he found himself a new hotel and a new girlfriend who he's probably lying to like he lied to me."

"Men like that are predators," Antoine said with a touch of indignation.

"Women like me are foolish," Beth replied wryly. "I should have asked more questions, checked him out before getting involved with him. I was stupid just to take everything he told me about himself at face value."

One thing surprised her, talking about Mark didn't bring the pain she'd expected. She realized that whatever heartbreak he might have caused her had finally healed.

"Beth, you can't blame yourself for being a trusting, loving woman. Those are very positive traits for a person to have, they are the very traits that draw me to you."

She pulled her hand from his. "Now that's enough about me. Why don't you tell me why you haven't found a woman to make your princess?"

"I will never marry." His voice rang with firm commitment.

She looked at him in surprise. "But why? Antoine, you're a good man and you deserve someone to share your life with." Not that she believed in a million years that woman could ever be her.

His eyes, which had been warm and inviting just moments ago, turned to pale ice.

"I'm not a good man, Beth. I've done some terrible things in my life, things that I fear might put your life in danger."

Chapter Six

Her beautiful eyes widened at his words. "What are you talking about?"

He looked toward the Sahron house and frowned. "You say this woman is scheduled to work at the hotel early in the morning?"

"Yes, she should be in by seven. She's never been late and never missed a day of work."

"Then let's go to your place. I'm in the mood for some peace and quiet and a cup of your wonderful coffee."

She said nothing but started the engine and headed out of the neighborhood. He knew she had questions about what he'd said, but he didn't intend to share any of his past with her until they were alone at her place.

He'd already had a difficult day. Thoughts of his friend Amir had plagued him, along with questions about the crash and the shooting he and Beth had experienced.

All day long he'd played and replayed the events in minute detail in his head. What he couldn't make sense of was that after he and Beth had crawled out of the wreck, the gunman had shot at her when she'd stood to go back into the car and get their cell phones.

Why shoot at her? If Antoine had been the primary target, then why not wait for him to stand up and then take him out? The shot at Beth had served as a warning to him. Had it simply been an amateur mistake or something else, something darker and more devious?

The more he thought about it, the more concerned he'd become that it was possibly somebody from his past who had caught up with him, somebody with a burning need for revenge who had finally found him.

And that meant he might have put a target on Beth's head. By spending time with her,

perhaps being seen in her company somebody might have gotten the impression that
she would make a good vehicle for revenge
against him. That was the only thing that
explained the gunman shooting at her instead of waiting for a bead on Antoine.

Darkness was falling fast as they reached
Beth's cabin. Antoine felt the same welcome
this evening as he had the other time he'd
come here with her. The house seemed to
attempt to embrace him in a serene quiet
but his mind was filled with too much chaos
for that to happen.

"I'm going to get out of my uniform,"
Beth said as she headed down the hallway.
"I'll be out in just a few minutes. Make
yourself at home."

He didn't hang around in the living room
but instead walked into the kitchen, where
Beth's presence in the house was most vi-
brant.

He walked over to the bank of windows
and stared out where the deep purple shadows of night were starting to pool beneath
the trees and seep across the land.

In the distance he could see the faint sparkle of the dying sun on a stream. Despite all the troubles in his mind, he momentarily felt a peace he rarely enjoyed.

This place had a rugged beauty that called to something deep inside him. From its jagged mountains to the sparkling streams, he felt an elemental pull, a sense of being where he belonged.

Which was crazy. He belonged in Barajas, he reminded himself. That was his home, not this place.

"Now, coffee."

He turned at the sound of her voice. She'd changed into a dark pink sweatshirt and a matching pair of jogging pants. The fleece material hugged her body like a lover and the peace he'd felt earlier dissolved beneath a wash of desire that threatened to weaken his knees.

He sank down at the table, disturbed by how profoundly Beth affected him, by how much he wanted her. He'd always been able to manage his emotions, his desires with little trouble. He was a master at manipulating others, but had always managed to stay completely in control of himself.

Until now.

Until Beth.

He narrowed his gaze as he watched her start the coffee. She moved with an efficient grace, despite her earlier claim of possessing two left feet.

"I tortured people." The words slipped from his lips, as if he knew these thoughts alone would drive any desire for her from his mind, would drive her away from him.

She gasped and turned to face him. He saw the nerve ticking violently in the side of her long, slender neck, letting him know she was anxious.

"What are you talking about?" Her voice was a soft whisper as she walked across the hardwood floor and sank down in the chair next to him.

He saw no fear in her eyes, only confusion and questions. The coffeemaker gurgled and began to drip its fragrant brew, but a cup of coffee was the last thing on his mind.

"It's what I did in the military," he said.

"I was one of the top interrogators for my country. I broke people, sometimes mentally, sometimes physically."

The darkness that was never far from the surface rose up inside him, filling him with the bitter tang of regret and a weight of sorrow he felt as if he'd never climb out from under. He was a thirty-five-year-old man who suffered nightmares because of his past. "I did terrible things, things that haunt me now."

"Antoine, you were in the military." She leaned toward him, her green eyes lit with the flame of conviction and holding a faint sense of redemption for him if he were willing to take it. "You were in charge of the security of your nation. You did what you had to do for your country," she said softly.

Unable to stand the easy acceptance in her eyes, he stood and returned to the window, his back to where she remained seated.

"I hate what I did." He spit the words out as his emotions careened out of control. "I hate who I had to become to get the job done. I found weaknesses and exploited them, I smiled with friendliness as I sought ways to destroy people, to break them to the point that I could get what I wanted from them."

He hadn't heard her rise from her chair, but suddenly her hand was on the small of his back. "The fact that you hate what you did shows me what kind of a man you are in your heart." Her soft voice soothed some of the rough edges in his soul.

He turned to face her. "It's what I dream about sometimes. It's the stuff of nightmares."

She tilted her head slightly and he realized the pulse in her neck had stopped its frantic beat. "Is that what you were dreaming about the night that I woke you up?"

He gave her a curt nod. "That and my parents' murder. Most of my nightmares are either of their murder or about the things I did in the name of national security."

"Antoine, you can't change what happened to your parents and you can't beat yourself up for doing your job for your country. You have to find a way to forgive yourself, to understand that you did what you had to do."

He wanted to fall into the softness of her green eyes, wanted desperately to believe he was the kind of man she thought him to be. She was so naïve, so accepting of not just his positive traits, but also of the dark side he'd tried to keep hidden from the world, from himself.

"What you don't understand is that I've made plenty of enemies. There are people out there who would like nothing better than to make me pay for what I did to them, or to their family members."

She frowned. "And you think that's who attacked us and not somebody out to destroy the coalition?" Her green eyes darkened slightly.

"I think it's possible and I also think it's possible they believe the way to hurt me is to hurt you."

"But why? I'm not your family." Her cheeks bloomed a dusty rose. "I'm just head of housekeeping at the hotel where you happen to be staying. I've just helped you out with some personal things."

"You know you're more than that to me," he said gruffly.

"But how would anyone else know what kind of a relationship you and I have?"

He led her back to the table and they both sat once again. "Somebody obviously saw us leave the hotel together, or as we drove to Jane's lab. Perhaps they drew certain conclusions about us being together in a more intimate way."

A frown once again sliced across her forehead. "But what makes you think it's somebody from your past?"

"There was no way the attack on us was done by professionals. It was clumsy and wrought with potential for errors. We could have seen the face of the driver, he might have wrecked his own vehicle in the process of trying to wreck ours. There were too many variables that could have made things go wrong. If he was trying to kill me after we got out of the crash, he shot too soon."

"He shot at me instead of you." Her voice

was flat, as if she was just now starting to believe what he was trying to tell her.

"If it had been a professional wanting to stop my participation in the COIN coalition, he would have waited until I stood to fire his first shot. That way I would have been clueless about his presence…and very dead."

The nerve in her neck reappeared and began to beat more distinctly and he reached out and tenderly placed a finger against the pulse. "Beth, I don't want to scare you, but I thought you should know that I might have brought danger to you."

Her eyes were amazingly soft as she gazed at him. "Then we'll just have to deal with it," she said.

A hardness that had been around his heart cracked apart and fell away. "That means I don't want you staying here alone." He moved his hand from the throbbing muscle in her throat and reached up and stroked a strand of her silky blond hair. "That means I don't even want you out of my sight."

"We'll figure it out," she replied, her voice a little breathless.

As he continued to look at her, his brain whirled with suppositions. If somebody was after her because they thought she was his lover, there was no real way to disabuse them of that notion.

He'd already made her a target and the best he could hope for was that he could keep her safe until he returned to Barajas. He felt confident that once he was out of the country the threat would follow him.

But for tonight he didn't intend to go anywhere. And all he could think about was that they had been damned by what they weren't doing—so why not go ahead and do it? Why not become her lover?

He stood once again and took her by the hand and pulled her up from her chair. He was immediately surrounded by the delicious scent of her that was as much a welcome as the aura of her home.

"The coffee is ready," she murmured as he drew her into his arms. Her body warmth radiated through the soft, fleece material.

"Hmm, suddenly I'm not in the mood for coffee." He leaned down and touched his lips to the warm flesh of her neck, then nibbled at the skin just beneath her ear. He felt the quickened beat of her heart against his and a faint tremor that stole through her. "I think it's time I made good on that earlier promise."

She didn't ask what promise he was talking about, rather she drew a shuddery breath and took him by the hand and led him down the hall toward her bedroom.

IT WAS LIKE A DREAM and she didn't ever want to wake up. Antoine's hand was warm and firm around hers as she led him into her bedroom.

This time it wasn't fear that caused her heart to crash wildly in her chest. It was a heady anticipation. She felt as if despite her internal protests to the contrary, they had been headed to this place when she'd first entered his suite after finding the notes in Amir's room.

They had danced around each other with

sensual intent every moment they had spent in each other's company and finally it was time for them to reward themselves with a payoff.

She dropped his hand and walked over to the nightstand and turned on the light. A soft spill of illumination filled the room and in the glow she saw the ravenous hunger that lit his pale eyes as he gazed at her.

Waves of heat swept over her as her mouth went dry. The look in his eyes was like an exquisite form of foreplay. He didn't even have to touch her for her to feel him on her skin, deep inside her.

"Are you sure?" His voice was deeper than usual as he stood at military attention at the foot of the bed.

It was the first time since she'd known him that he appeared the least bit uncertain and that only made her more sure of what she wanted from him.

She walked to where he stood and laced her arms around his neck. "I want you to hold me, Antoine. I want you to kiss me until neither of us can think of anything but each other. I want you to make love with me and then hold me tight until morning comes."

Blue flames shot from his eyes. "I can do that starting right now." His mouth feathered over hers in a surprisingly light kiss that teased her senses and made her yearn for more...so very much more.

He wrapped his arms around her back and pulled her close and she didn't know if the rapidly beating heart she felt was his or her own.

His mouth blazed a trail down her jaw and to her neck, where his lips lightly nipped at the sensitive skin just below her ear.

She'd expected command and he gave her a gentleness that stole her breath away. "Sweet Beth," he whispered softly. "You are absolutely amazing."

He made her feel amazing, like she was the brightest, the sexiest woman in the world. Nobody had ever made her feel the way Antoine did and she had a feeling that nobody would again. This moment was magic. This man was magic and she wanted to savor it forever.

When his lips took hers again in a fiery kiss she was ready to rip her clothes off and get beneath the covers with him. But he seemed to be in no hurry. Languidly his hands stroked up and down her back as his mouth continued to ply hers with heat.

She didn't want to think about what would happen when they left the bed in the morning. He was a hotel guest and had a country to return to and she knew in the very depths of her heart he would leave without her.

She would go back to being the highly efficient head of housekeeping with nothing but memories to keep her warm. But even knowing that she wanted him.

Perhaps someday in the distant future she could tell her grandchildren about the time she had shared with a handsome prince whose life had been in danger. Of course, she wouldn't tell them about this night of desire, but she'd tell them how she'd helped him in his quest to save his life and the lives of his friends.

All thoughts of grandchildren fled out of her mind. There was only Antoine and his fiery lips and the smooth slide of his hands down her back.

He finally released his hold on her and stepped back. As she stood frozen in place he leaned down and removed the gun that had been strapped to his ankle. He placed it on the nightstand, along with his wallet, and then began to unbutton his shirt.

With each button that was unfastened more of his dark, muscled chest was revealed. Beth felt her knees weaken as he finally shrugged the shirt off and it fell to the floor behind him. Taut chest muscles and six-pack abs attested to the fact that he was a man who worked out regularly.

It was only then that he approached her again. "You look adorable in that pink sweatshirt, but I have a need now to take it off you." The fact that he'd spoken his intent out loud only made her hotter.

Her heart hitched in her chest as he took

the bottom of the shirt and effortlessly pulled it over her head and then threw it into one of the darkened corners of the room. She desperately wished she was wearing a sexy black or red lacy bra instead of the white cotton.

"Beautiful," he whispered.

She splayed her hands across his hard chest and smiled up at him. "Beautiful," she agreed as the heat of him warmed her palms.

"Do you have any idea how crazy you make me?" His fingers trailed a path across her bare collarbone.

"It can't be any more crazy than you make me," she replied breathlessly. "Antoine, nobody has ever made me feel the way you do."

He moved his fingers from her collarbone to her cheek. "I like that…and now I think we've talked enough."

She released a delighted gasp as he swept her up into his arms and carried her to the bed. He lay her down and then sat next to her and removed the slippers she'd put on when she'd changed out of her uniform.

When her slippers were gone he took the waistband of her jogging pants and pulled and she raised her hips to help him remove them.

Her heart now thundered as he once again stood and kicked off his shoes and then moved his hands to the waistband of his slacks. He hesitated. "Are you still sure about this? I need you to be sure, Beth. I don't want regrets from you, now or ever."

"I've never been so sure of anything in my life," she replied fervently. It was true. Right or wrong, she was going to make love to him tonight.

With surprisingly graceful movements, he took off his slacks, exposing black briefs beneath and long, muscular legs. He was perfection and the sight of him nearly naked only served to increase her desire for him.

As he joined her on the bed their legs wrapped together with the comfortable ease of longtime lovers. Their bodies fit perfectly, like yin and yang symbols.

Kisses became caresses and it wasn't long before both of them were impatient with the underwear that kept them separate. As he removed her bra his mouth eagerly covered one of her nipples.

She felt the pull of his lips deep in the pit of her stomach as her nipple responded to his touch, pebbling into a hard knot. She tightened her hands on his shoulders, loving the play of his muscles beneath her fingers.

He teased the tip of her nipple with his tongue, first licking and then nipping until she was gasping with the fiery sensations that coursed through her. Her blood was hot in her veins and she wanted more...more of him.

Within minutes the last of their clothing was gone and his hot caresses seemed to be everywhere...across the swollen rise of her breasts, down the flat of her stomach and whispering softly on her inner thighs until she wanted to scream with her need of him.

"I love the little sound you make in the back of your throat when I stroke you here," he whispered as he once again ran his hot, wicked fingers lightly over the inside of her thigh.

"And what kind of a sound do you make when I touch you here?" She moved her hand slowly down his stomach and encircled his hardness. A small moan escaped his lips and she smiled. "I like that sound."

"You are a wanton woman, Beth, and if you aren't careful this will be over long before I want it to be." Gently he shoved her hand from him and instead touched her where she most wanted him.

Instantly she tensed with pleasure. His fingers were magic and she felt the swell of not only her physical reaction to his touch but also the surge of emotion that accompanied her impending release.

Tears misted her eyes as the waves built up…up and then finally came crashing all around her and she cried out his name over and over again.

"Please," she said when she'd managed to catch half her breath. She knew she was begging but she didn't care. She wanted him fully, wanted him to possess her completely. "Please, Antoine, take me now."

He rolled over toward the nightstand and grabbed his wallet and withdrew a condom. A small relief flooded through her. She hadn't even thought about protection.

With the condom in place he moved between her thighs and entered her with an agonizing slowness that spiraled her upward once again.

When he was deep within her, she clung to his shoulders as she moved her hips to meet his thrusts. She was glad they'd left the light on, so that she could see the hunger in his eyes as he plunged into her faster and faster.

Suddenly he slowed and nearly stopped moving. She bucked beneath him as her well of want grew bigger. He smiled down at her and then resumed his movements.

He teased and tormented her, bringing her almost to the brink and then stopping. She could tell by the taut cords in his neck that he was teasing not only her, but himself as well.

She tightened around him, and saw his control snap with the blaze of his eyes. Wildly he moved against her, groans of pleasure escaping his lips.

She cried out his name as she shuddered with another climax. He stiffened against her in response as he found his own.

They clung to each other, breathless for several long moments. He finally got up and went into the bathroom while Beth remained sated and boneless beneath the sheets. When he returned, he turned off the light on the nightstand and then got back into bed and pulled her against him.

She snuggled into the warmth of his body, feeling safer, more content that she could ever remember feeling. He stroked her hair and pressed his lips against her forehead.

"That was amazing," he said in a soft whisper.

"You were amazing," she murmured drowsily.

"We were amazing together," he replied with a satisfied laugh.

She burrowed closer against his chest and

as sleep reached out to claim her, she tried not to think about the fact that Prince Antoine Cavanaugh of Barajas was definitely going to break her heart.

Chapter Seven

They got up and drank a cup of coffee and shared a piece of cake together, giggling like teenagers in the middle of the night.

Antoine entertained her with stories about his and Sebastian's childhood antics, loving the sound of her laughter and the way amusement sparkled in her eyes.

He thought it possible that he could have a lifetime of her laughter and never tire of the sound. "You had a happy childhood?" he asked.

"I had a wonderful childhood," she replied. "The woods were my playground and before my mother got ill we spent lots of time exploring. We'd have wonderful picnics when the weather was nice."

"And you'd prepare gourmet food for the occasion?" he asked.

She smiled and shook her head. "I really didn't start getting interested in cooking until after my mother was ill. Her appetite wasn't good and so I started trying new recipes to tempt her. That's what led to my love of cooking."

When the cake was gone and her eyelids were drooping with sleepiness, they turned out all the lights in the house and got back into bed.

She cuddled up beside him and he stroked her hair, more at peace than he could ever remember being. He could hear a faint night breeze through the window that tinkled the wind chime, and a rhythmic clicking from some kind of insect. The sounds only added to the peace that invaded his soul.

"Antoine, I know you said you'd never marry, but have you never wanted children?" Beth asked softly.

He hesitated a long moment before replying. "I never thought much about children until I spent time with Samantha Peters."

His heart softened as he thought of the four-year-old little girl who would eventually call him Uncle. "She was quite a little charmer and I must confess for a moment I wondered what it might be like to have a child of my own. But, just like I have no place in my life for a wife, there's no place in my life for children."

"That's sad," she said softly. "You would make a wonderful father, Antoine."

He tried not to allow her words to ache in his heart. What kind of father would he make always looking over his shoulder, always worried that somehow, someway his enemies would find him? "What about you? You want children?"

"Definitely. At least two and I want them to know the kind of love my mother showed me." She snuggled closer against him and within minutes he knew she'd fallen asleep.

Antoine remained awake long after Beth had fallen asleep, watching her in the faint spill of moonlight that fell into the window.

He loved the feel of her in his arms. He hadn't expected making love to her to fill him with such a depth of emotion. He'd thought she'd be like all the other women he'd had in his life, easy to make love to and just as easy to walk away from and forget.

Was this how his father had felt about his mother?

Had his father known the danger of loving her but been unable to stop himself? Had he fought what he felt with all his might, only to realize that love was stronger than fear?

Surely what Antoine felt wasn't love. It was simply the pleasure of their lovemaking that had him feeling such craziness. He'd spent his entire life telling himself that his heart was not meant to love.

Perhaps his feelings for Beth were tied up with the fact that he had nobody else he could trust, that she provided a safe haven of sorts from the madness that had become his life here in the United States.

Perhaps it was time for him to consider returning to Barajas. He wasn't really accomplishing anything in his mission to find Amir. The COIN summit had been canceled and he certainly wouldn't be making any trade deals while he was here. That would happen at another place, at another time.

Was it time to go home? A tiny bit of rebellion burned in his belly at the thought. There had been times over the last three weeks that he'd considered not going back to Barajas. Sebastian was perfectly capable of carrying the leadership of the nation alone and Antoine had never truly been comfortable beneath the mantle of responsibility.

He loved this wild and beautiful state he'd found himself in, loved the idea of being a cowboy and settling into a different kind of lifestyle. But, he also wondered if this wasn't just a need to escape the intrigue that had surrounded him for the past couple of weeks.

Closing his eyes he breathed in the sweet scent of Beth and told himself that no matter what happened he couldn't love her. He was the master of his emotions, in total control of his feelings and he absolutely, positively refused to allow himself to love her.

He drifted off to sleep and the dream came almost immediately. Big, muscular men clad all in black surrounded the bed where he and Beth lay, their dark eyes filled with intense hatred, with the bloodthirsty need for revenge.

Antoine could smell their rage in the room, an acrid scent that let him know they were dangerous, that he and Beth were in terrible trouble.

"You took my father's pride and he died a broken man," one of them said. "He was a farmer and had nothing to do with politics."

"You stole my brother's honor and now you're going to pay," another exclaimed.

All the men began to shout and Antoine found himself powerless to respond, unable to move a single muscle. Beth remained sleeping next to him, unaware of the danger that surrounded them.

Panic seared up the back of his throat as he struggled to respond. But, his efforts were to no avail, he remained mute and motionless, unable to defend himself or Beth against the attack.

"You took from us and now we'll take from you." One of the men gazed at Beth as he pulled a long, wicked knife from his belt.

Agony screamed through Antoine's head as he realized they intended to hurt her. *Kill me,* he silently screamed. *I'm the one who broke your father. I'm the one who hurt your brother. Take me and leave her alone!*

He awakened with a start and bolted up, gasping for air as he gazed around the moonlit room. Alone. He and Beth were alone in the room. There were no men hovering next to the bed, nobody in the shadows. It had all just been a terrible nightmare.

He raked a hand down his face and drew several deep breaths. A cold sweat chilled him as the last of the horror of the dream faded away.

With a sigh he lay back down and looked at Beth, who was curled up on her side and still sleeping soundly. His heart crunched painfully in his chest.

He felt as if by involving her in his little investigation he'd damned her. By merely being in his presence he'd made somebody believe that she was important enough to him to be used as a weapon against him.

He didn't believe in the prophecy of dreams, but there was no question that the nightmare he'd just suffered had the aura of a warning. The problem was he felt as if it was too late to change anything where Beth was concerned. The dream and his knowledge of what had happened to his father only made him more certain that he would never have a woman, not even Beth, as a permanent part of his life.

Closing his eyes he tried to find sleep again, praying that it would be a slumber without visions, that if there were dreams they would be happy ones.

He had to believe that Amir would be found alive, that the rest of the coalition would be okay and that Beth would be all right when he eventually returned to Barajas.

He'd just about fallen back to sleep when he thought he heard the faint tinkle of breaking glass.

He froze. Was it part of a new dream? Or a trick of his imagination? Had the wind picked up and what he'd heard was the wind chime outside the window? There was no repeat of the noise that would make him believe it was simply the wind.

He tried to relax but after a moment sat up once again, knowing that he wouldn't be able to go back to sleep until he went to investigate what had made the noise.

Silently he slid out of the bed and pulled on his briefs and his slacks, then grabbed his gun from the nightstand, his heart beating unsteadily as he made his way out of the bedroom.

He paused in the darkened hallway and listened, and heard a faint sound he couldn't identify. He took several more steps and ahead he could see a faint flickering light coming from the kitchen area.

What the hell? He frowned and gripped the gun tighter in his hand as he entered the living room. He'd gotten halfway through the room when the acrid air reached his nose and he saw the dark swirl of smoke that waved ghostly fingers in front of the windows.

Fire!

The word exploded in his head in alarm. Shielding his nose and mouth with the back of his hand, he entered the kitchen. One of the breakfast nook windows was broken and fire danced up the curtains and ate at the wooden wall.

He smelled the distinct scent of gasoline and guessed that a Molotov cocktail had been thrown through the window and had exploded.

Dammit! Somebody must have followed them here. He'd assumed with the new vehicle they wouldn't be noticed for at least a couple of days.

He coughed as the viscous black smoke thickened, not only obscuring his visibility but also invading his lungs. They had to get out of the house. With the wooden structure to feed it, the fire would be completely out of control within minutes.

He raced back to the bedroom and flipped

on the overhead light. "Beth, get up." He ran
to the side of the bed and pulled at her arm.

She gazed at him in sleepy confusion.
"What? What's wrong?"

"Quickly, put some clothes on. The house
is on fire. We have to get out of here," he
exclaimed.

The sleepiness instantly left her eyes. She
jumped out of bed but instead of grabbing
for her clothes, she reached for the phone on
the nightstand and called 911 to report the
fire. Only then did she grab the sweatshirt
and sweatpants and pull them on.

By this time the smoke had snaked down
the hallway and had begun to drift into the
bedroom. He shoved his gun into his waistband and stepped into his shoes while she
pulled on her sneakers. He was aware that
every second they wasted meant the fire
was getting bigger, hungrier and the danger
to them grew more intense.

"We should be able to get out the front
door," he said as he took her by the hand
and pulled her out of the bedroom. He got
them halfway to the front door when he

halted, his brain working to process the entire situation.

"Wait!" He stopped her from opening the front door as his brain snapped and fired. It was a perfect ruse. Set a fire in the rear of the house and then wait for the occupants to run out the front door. It would be easy to pick them off as they came out of the door.

"We can't go out that way," he exclaimed.

Thankfully she didn't take time to question his words. "The back door," she replied and started to tug him toward the kitchen.

He remained grounded and shook his head and then realized she probably couldn't see the action through the thick smoke that surrounded them. "It's too dangerous. The fire is near the back door." Besides, he had no idea if more than one person might be waiting outside for them.

Her hand clutched his in a death grip. "How do we get out?" she cried and then was taken over by a violent spasm of coughing.

"Come on." He pulled her back down the hallway and into the main bathroom where he closed the door behind them. "Don't turn on the light," he cautioned her. He didn't want to alert anyone outside as to exactly where they were in the house.

"Somebody is out there, aren't they?" she whispered. He felt her frightened gaze on him as he opened the bathroom window. When he turned to face her, she was barely visible in the faint moonlight that spilled into the window.

He placed his palms on either side of her face, his heart racing with a rush of adrenaline. His only desire at that moment was to keep her safe.

"Somebody *is* out there," he replied with a sense of urgency. "I think they set the fire and now they're just waiting for us to leave the house. We can't stay inside, the smoke is getting thicker and it's too dangerous."

She opened her mouth as if to say something, but he slid his finger over her lips to still her. "They will be expecting us to go out either the front or the back door. I'm hoping we can get out this window without being detected."

She nodded and he pulled his finger away from her mouth. "I'm going to go out first and you follow me. Once you hit the ground don't wait for me and don't look back. Just run like your life depends on it, because I'm afraid that it does."

Without waiting for a response, he slid his head out the window and looked around. Nobody. He saw nobody lurking in the darkness. He raised himself up and over the window ledge and dropped silently to the ground.

Gun firmly in hand, he once again scanned the area and then motioned Beth to climb out. Just as he'd instructed, she hit the ground and headed for the trees, not looking back as she ran.

He tightened his grip on his gun and went into a crouch position as he began to move along the side of the house and gave one last look toward the trees, praying this wasn't the very last time he'd see Beth.

SHE RAN THROUGH THE TREES like a rabid animal, darting first one way and then another as terror kept any rational thought out of her head.

Ladybug, ladybug, fly away home. Your house is on fire and your children all gone.

The nursery rhyme repeated itself over and over again in her head and she felt a burst of hysterical laughter rise to her lips.

But she swallowed it, unsure who might be hiding behind a bush, who might be in the shadows of the night waiting to discern her location.

Who had seen them? Had somebody been hiding in the woods, watching her cabin and hoping to catch them here? On the drive she'd checked her rearview often, but had seen nobody following behind them. How had this happened? What would happen next?

She finally collapsed at the base of a tree and held her breath, listening for the sound of Antoine, for the sound of anyone who might be near. A stitch in her side burned painfully, but she ignored it.

Where was Antoine right now? Was he hiding in the trees or had he gone chasing the danger? She feared the latter and the only thing that made her feel the slightest bit better was that she hadn't heard the sound of any gunfire…at least not yet.

She didn't even want to think about her house…her home. It was just stuff, she told herself, and she didn't need stuff. What she needed was for Antoine to be okay. The last thing she wanted was for him to try to be a hero. Dead heroes held no appeal except in history books.

He had to be all right. She sent a dozen prayers toward the sky, praying for Antoine's safety. It would be tragic if anything happened to him, tragic for her and for all the people of Barajas.

Her heart banged so loudly in her chest she wasn't sure she'd hear if anyone snuck up behind her. Even though she was on the ground every muscle in her body was tensed for flight.

Who had done this? Was it somebody from Antoine's past, like he suspected? There was no doubt that this act had been meant to hurt not just him, but her as well.

She sensed true hatred behind this, a hatred that went beyond political goals and into something far more personal.

Her heart leaped at the sound of sirens in the distance. Help was coming! She pulled herself back up to her feet and began to silently move in the direction of the cabin.

She hid behind a stand of trees that gave her a perfect view of the house and as she saw the flames eating at the kitchen, tears welled up in her eyes.

The kitchen, the place where she'd spent many happy hours. Had the fire broken the cookie jar that had belonged to her grandmother, burned the cookbooks that had been handed down through the generations? Had the dish towels her mother embroidered turned to char?

At that moment strong arms encircled her from behind and a hand shot over her mouth to still the scream that begged to escape.

"It's me," Antoine's voice whispered in her ear just as she was ready to whirl around and fight for her life.

He released his hold on her and she

turned and threw herself into his arms. The tears she'd shoved back finally spilled from her eyes as he held her close.

Their heartbeats raced against each other as they clung together. "I was so afraid," she finally managed to gasp. "I was so afraid for you."

His arms tightened around her. "We'll be safe now. Sheriff Wolf is here."

The clearing around the house had become filled with firemen, lawmen and equipment. By the time she and Antoine left the cover of the trees the fire was under control and nearly out, although smoke still lingered in the air.

Jake Wolf stood near the back of the house, talking to the fire chief as they approached. When he spied them he left the man and came over to talk to them.

"Thank God you both got out safely," he said. He looked as tired as Beth felt. Soot dusted his high cheekbones and his eyes held a weariness. It seemed like an eternity since Beth had been sleeping peacefully in Antoine's arms.

"What happened?" Jake asked.

"We were sleeping and I woke up when I heard breaking glass. I got up to investigate and found the kitchen on fire. I think perhaps it was a Molotov cocktail that broke the window." Antoine placed an arm around Beth's shoulder. "We managed to get out through the bathroom window. I told Beth to hide in the woods and I went to investigate."

Jake's features tightened. "Prince Antoine, I would prefer you leave the investigating to me."

"In any case I didn't see anyone," Antoine replied, but it was obvious by his voice that he wished he had seen somebody.

Jake looked at Antoine and then at Beth and she felt the unspoken questions the sheriff had. She tried not to feel embarrassed about the fact that it would probably now be obvious to Jake that she and Antoine were in an intimate relationship.

"Are you okay?" Jake asked her, his gaze uncharacteristically soft.

"I'm fine," she replied and fought a new

wave of tears as she looked at the house. Even though she'd told herself it was just things and not important, they had been *her* things and the fact that somebody had willfully destroyed them both made her angry and made her want to weep.

"It's not as bad as it looks," Jake said, as if reading her thoughts.

"I have insurance," she replied and stiffened her shoulders. "I'm sure it will all be okay."

Jake looked back at Antoine. "We'll know more tomorrow when things cool down and the fire chief can get inside and take a look around. In the meantime me and some of my men will search the area and see what we can find. I'll also make sure somebody stays here on the property until arrangements can be made for Beth to return."

"Thanks, Sheriff. Can we go?" Antoine asked. "It's been a bad night and Beth needs to be someplace safe."

"I'll have a deputy drive you back to the hotel and another one to drive your car back there," Jake replied. "But I'm sure I'll have more questions for you in the morning."

Minutes later they were in the back of a patrol car. Beth could smell the acrid scent of smoke that clung to them as she leaned against Antoine's side.

"Try not to worry," he said softly. "I'll do whatever it takes to fix things."

"Insurance will take care of it," she replied wearily. It wasn't his job to fix things for her. He'd already bought her a new vehicle and she absolutely refused to accept anything else from him.

They were silent for the remainder of the ride back to the hotel, where the deputy insisted he accompany them to Antoine's suite. Thankfully at this hour of the morning the lobby was empty except for a few members of the staff who were cleaning the area.

They watched openmouthed as the three walked through and down the hallway that led to the suite. Beth could only imagine the gossip that would roar through the place in the next couple of hours. At the moment she was too tired to care. She'd deal with it in the morning.

A second deputy appeared to hand them the keys to the Jeep and then they were left alone. Beth stood in the middle of the living room area, unsure what her next move should be.

She was beyond numb. It had all been too much, the car crash, the bullets and now the fire. She was simply overwhelmed by it all.

"Come." Antoine took her by the hand and led her into the master bathroom. He started the water in the huge, glass-enclosed shower and then turned back to her and began to undress her.

Gently he pulled the smoky, soot-covered sweatshirt over her head and tossed it to the floor. When he pulled down her pants, she stepped out of them, still numb to the world.

There was nothing sexual about his actions. It was only tenderness she felt, along with his obvious need to take care of her. And she let him, grateful that she didn't have to think, didn't have to do anything but submit to him.

When they were both naked he pulled her into the warm spray of water. Using the clean-scented soap the hotel provided he quickly washed and rinsed himself and then began to wash her.

He dragged the soap-filled sponge over her shoulders and down her chest. She stood impassive and merely accepted, like a child being washed by a parent. He washed every inch of her until she was slicked with soap.

When he was finished he pulled her back beneath the warm spray and she closed her eyes as the scent of smoke finally disappeared down the drain. With her body cleaned, he used the shampoo and began to wash her hair.

She leaned with her bare chest and face pressed against one wall of the shower, the glass warm as she dropped her head back. His fingers worked against her scalp in a hypnotic fashion. Her brain was emptied of all thoughts as she completely gave herself to his care.

Slowly, she felt herself beginning to relax,

leaving behind the terror that had filled her through the long, seemingly endless night.

By the time he was finished and her hair had been rinsed until it squeaked with cleanliness, she was beyond exhaustion. He turned off the shower, dried himself and pulled on one of the thick robes the resort provided, then dried her off and pulled his own robe around her.

She reveled in the scent of him that clung to the robe. It smelled like caring. It smelled like safety. He then picked her up and carried her into the bedroom where the bed had been turned down and was ready for sleep.

"I should make arrangements to return to Barajas and take you with me," he said once they were in the bed, with his body spooned around hers and his arm around her waist. "I feel responsible for you and there I can arrange for your safety without problems."

"Let's discuss it in the morning," she said and squeezed her eyes as tears once again burned. For in that moment she realized she didn't need him to fix her house. She didn't want to be his responsibility. The only thing she really wanted was for Antoine to love her.

Chapter Eight

Antoine awoke and knew by the cast of the sun slanting in through the windows that it was late morning. For several long moments he remained in the warm bed, reluctant to leave the comfort and the faint scent of Beth that filled the air.

He glanced over to the other side of the bed where she was curled up facing him. Her features were soft and his fingers ached with the desire to touch her cheek, to awaken her with a sweet kiss and then make love to her while her body was soft and warm and yielding.

She'd lost so much because of him. And last night she could have lost her life.

He fought his impulse to reach over and draw her into his embrace, repeat the lovemaking that had blown his mind. She deserved her sleep after all she'd been through.

But, it didn't take long before he grew restless, knowing that there were many things to attend to and staying in bed wouldn't accomplish anything. With Beth still soundly sleeping, he slid from the bed, grabbed his robe and left the room.

The meeting with the housekeeper Janine Sahron would have to wait until later in the day. He knew there would be much business concerning the events of the night before to take care of this morning.

The first thing he did was order coffee and breakfast from room service and then arranged for housekeeping to dispose of the smoky clothing they'd worn the night before. Finally, he called the gift shop and ordered a pair of slacks and a blouse for Beth to put on when she awakened.

With the immediate needs taken care of, he sank down in one of the leather chairs by the fireplace and replayed the night's events in his head.

Why hadn't he considered that they might be in danger at her cabin? Had he allowed his overwhelming desire for her, his need to get her alone and make love to her to completely muddy his brain?

It was the only explanation for his foolish judgment and he hated himself for it. He'd allowed himself to be ruled by his emotions and that had nearly gotten them killed. It was definitely a mistake he wouldn't allow to happen again.

He could only hope that either the fire chief or Jake Wolf would be able to find some clue in the ruins of Beth's cabin that might lead them to arrest the person responsible for this latest attack.

He still believed the attacks he and Beth had suffered were too amateurish to be part of a bigger conspiracy with professional players in the mix.

Verovick wouldn't have used a Molotov cocktail, when he or his men could have planted an effective bomb in the car or in the house. There were any number of ways a professional killer could get to him without resorting to something as primitive as a gasoline-filled bottle stuffed with fabric.

Once again he suspected it was someone with a personal vendetta rather than anyone connected with the COIN coalition.

Who could it be? Who had the resources to follow him across the sea with the sole purpose of revenge? He didn't know how to begin to identify a person or persons who might be behind all this.

Dammit, he should have never pulled Beth into his drama. He should have insisted he take the notes from her and then left her to go on her merry way.

One thing was certain. She would not be returning to her home. She would not be going anywhere anytime soon. She didn't know it yet, but he intended to make her a prisoner in this suite until he knew for sure that the danger to her was gone for good.

He jumped as his cell phone rang and answered to hear Sebastian's voice. "My brother, how are things in Barajas?" he asked.

"Very well," Sebastian replied. "Jessica

and little Samantha are settling in quite nicely and our people seem to be pleased that I finally have a woman by my side. What about there? Any news on Amir? Any other developments?"

"I'm afraid there's been nothing new on Amir," Antoine replied and then told his brother what had happened since last time they spoke. "I have a bad feeling, Sebastian. I don't think these attacks are related to our reason for being here in the States. I think it's somebody from my past and my biggest regret is that now I believe Beth is in danger as well."

The two brothers discussed what Antoine had learned about Verovick and speculated on the Russian mob's involvement in the conspiracy against the royals.

As he spoke with his brother, confessing all his concerns about Beth and how much his involvement with her had cost her, once again he was struck by her bravery. She was a woman unlike any other that he'd ever known. She would make some man a wonderful wife. She would be a courageous and beautiful mother and the fact that he wouldn't be around to see that broke his heart. The conversation was interrupted by a knock on the door.

"I think breakfast has arrived," Antoine said into the phone as he got up from his chair.

"Then I'll let you go and enjoy your food. Stay safe, Antoine."

"I'm doing my best, my brother," he replied.

"And keep in touch," Sebastian added. With a promise to do just that, Antoine hung up.

At the door was not only breakfast, but also an employee from the gift shop with the items he'd requested for Beth. As the meal was being set on the table, he carried the clothing into the bedroom where he discovered that Beth was out of bed and in the bathroom.

He knocked on the door. "Beth, I have some clean clothes here for you."

She opened the door and he saw that she'd neatly brushed her hair and her face was dewy with a recent scrub. She looked ach-ingly beautiful and for just a moment he wanted to pull her from the bathroom and back into the bed. He wanted to forget what had happened, not worry about what might happen and just hold her once again in his arms.

"Thank you," she said and took the clothes from him and then closed the bath-room door once again.

There had been a touch of distance in her eyes, he thought as he quickly got dressed for the day. And could he blame her? She'd simply offered to drive him where he wanted to go and now she'd lost a vehicle, her house had been damaged and her pri-vacy invaded.

He hadn't missed the shocked looks on the faces of the cleaning crew working in the lobby when he and Beth returned to the suite last night.

He knew the gossip that would be flying around the resort this morning, gossip about the prince and the head of housekeeping.

Long after he left here she would have to

deal with the aftermath of her involvement with him. He had brought her nothing but trouble, was it any wonder her eyes had held a distance?

He returned to the dining area and poured himself a cup of coffee and by that time Beth had joined him. The navy slacks he'd bought kissed the length of her legs with perfection. The peach-colored blouse brought out the blond highlights in her shoulder-length hair and the bright green of her eyes.

Had it only been the night before when he'd tasted the sweetness of her lips? Felt the burn of her body next to his? Desire once again nibbled at him, like a voracious hunger that refused to be ignored, a hunger that would never be completely satisfied.

"Thank you for the clothes," she said.

"I didn't think you'd want to put the soot-covered smoky things from last night back on."

"Have you heard anything from Jake this morning?" she asked as she poured herself a cup of coffee and took a seat at the table.

"Not yet. If I don't hear anything from him by the time we finish our meal, I'll call him." He joined her at the table. "I'm hoping he'll have some news for us."

"You ordered enough breakfast for an army," she observed.

He looked at the food on the table. There were pancakes and eggs, fresh fruit and oatmeal and biscuits and bagels. He looked back at her. "I woke up hungry."

She must have seen something in his eyes that let her know he was talking about more than just an appetite for breakfast. Her cheeks grew pink as she speared a pancake and placed it on her plate.

He watched as she took banana slices and placed them on the pancake like eyes, then used an orange slice to make a mouth on the pancake. She looked up to see him watching her and a small smile curved her lips.

"My mother used to do this to my pancakes when I was a little girl and was being crabby. She'd say, 'Look, Beth, your pancake is smiling at you and he wants a smile back.'" She looked at him and her cheeks were pink. "Silly, I know, but whenever I was upset it always worked to bring a smile to my face."

He hated that the implication was that she was upset now and had reached back into the memories of her childhood to feel better. Again he mentally cursed himself for getting her involved in his mess.

He sought words to comfort her, but recognized at the moment he had none. He couldn't tell her everything was going to be okay when he didn't know what to expect next. He refused to mouth empty platitudes. She deserved so much better than that.

"Do you have happy memories of your mother?" she asked as they began to eat.

The most easily accessed memory Antoine had of his mother, Nephra, was of the night of her death. Certainly not a happy one.

He now fought past that particularly horrific memory in an attempt to find others more pleasant from his earlier childhood.

And they were there, just waiting to be tapped into.

"She loved to sing," he said, surprised by the sudden recollection. "And she had the voice of an angel." His heart warmed as he thought about the lullabies his mother would sing to him and Sebastian before they drifted off to sleep each night.

And releasing that pleasant memory from his past prompted others to spring free. "I remember her taking Sebastian and me to the beach where we built sand castles and played in the waves. She loved the water and swam like a fish. She taught both Sebastian and me to swim. She had a laugh that could fill a room and she loved us and my father to distraction."

Beth laid a hand on his forearm. "Those are the memories you should dream about, Antoine. Embrace the love your parents had for you and for each other and let it be your place of dreams."

It was at that moment that he knew that the most difficult thing he'd ever do in his life was tell Beth Taylor goodbye.

JAKE WOLF ARRIVED at the suite at the same time they finished breakfast. Antoine gestured him into the living area where Jake sat on one of the chairs facing Antoine and Beth who were seated on the sofa.

Beth looked at him anxiously, knowing he'd probably spent the morning at her place. "How bad is it?" she asked.

"The good news is the fire damage was confined to the kitchen area," Jake said. "There is some mild smoke damage throughout but a good cleaning company should be able to take care of all that."

A touch of relief filtered through her. Pots and pans could be bought again and held no sentimental value. Of all the rooms in the house she could only be grateful that it had been the kitchen that had taken the brunt of the flames.

Jake turned his attention to Antoine. "You were right. It was a Molotov cocktail. We found pieces of the bottle near the window and gasoline was used as the accelerant."

"The type of bottle?" Antoine asked.

"An ordinary beer bottle that was loaded with gasoline and had what looks like part of a bed sheet as a wick," Jake replied. "We're hoping to pull some prints from the fragments of the bottle we collected." Jake looked formidable as his eyes narrowed. "If we lift a print, then I'll see to it that the person is behind bars for a long time to come. This wasn't a simple case of arson, it was definitely attempted murder. Whoever threw that bottle had to have known that you and Beth were in the house."

Antoine nodded, looking equally grim. "I have dispatched a couple of members of my security team to sit on the house and make sure there is no issue with looting. Beth will not be returning there until somebody is behind bars."

Jake nodded. "That seems like a wise idea to me."

"Hello?" Beth said in irritation. "I'm right here and I will make my own decisions." Both men turned to look at her. "And I won't be returning to the house until somebody is behind bars, although I would like to go there and pack some things."

"We also found some tire marks in an area near the house we think might belong to the perpetrator. We cast them and hopefully we'll be able to figure out exactly what kind of car it was," Jake added.

As the two men continued discussing all the events that had taken place over the last couple of days, Beth thought about what her next move should be.

The one thing she wouldn't do was pick up her life and go to Barajas where Antoine thought he could keep her safe. She wouldn't become a weighted ball around his neck, another responsibility he had to take care of. That was simply not an option.

She would stay in a room here in the hotel until her place was put back together. What she wouldn't do was stay in the suite with Antoine.

As crazy as it seemed in the short amount of time they'd spent together, she'd fallen in love with him, and now each minute that she remained with him only deepened her love. Somehow she had to cut her losses now, not get in any deeper than she already was.

She knew that when he left the country, when all this was said and done, she would be left with a heart that wasn't just bruised, but rather battered.

"If you'd like, I can take you to get your things from the house right now," Jake said, pulling Beth from her thoughts.

"That would be wonderful," she replied and stood.

"I'll go as well," Antoine said.

Beth shook her head. "No," she said firmly. "I'll be fine with Jake and he doesn't need to worry about both of us." She raised her chin slightly and held Antoine's gaze. She needed some time away, wanted to see the damage to her home without him there.

"I would prefer you remain here, Prince Antoine," Jake said.

Antoine hesitated another moment and then gave a curt nod of his head. "Very well, but I insist you return to my suite when you have your things," he said to Beth. "I need to know that you're safe and sound."

"Okay," she replied. It was easier to comply for now than to argue in front of Jake. But, she had no intention of spending another night in Antoine's bed, another night of wanting him and loving him.

It was time she get back to reality and the reality was Antoine had made it clear to her that he wasn't interested in marriage and babies. Although she knew without doubt that he cared about her, that he wanted her physically, she also knew there was no future with him.

Minutes later she was in Jake's car and headed to her house. "How are you holding up through all this?" he asked.

"I guess as well as can be expected," she replied. "I certainly didn't realize what I was getting myself into by becoming friendly with Antoine. What about you? Your workload has certainly been crazy since all this began."

He gave her a wry smile. "I've definitely had to stay on my toes." The smile fell from his face. "I've never felt such frustration as I have over the last several weeks. I have a missing sheik and can't seem to find a clue that might tell me what happened to him. I've got attacks happening on everyone and no real suspects."

"I don't think any of us will be the same when the royals return to their countries and life gets back to normal." She gazed out the side window. She'd certainly never be the same. There would always be memories of Antoine and at the moment she couldn't imagine ever loving another man.

"I'm not sure any of us will recognize normal when it does happen again," Jake replied drily.

Within minutes they were back at her cabin. As she got out of the car her heart constricted in her chest. A big, burly man stood at the front door and wore a uniform that identified him as part of the security Antoine had provided. He was definitely big enough that anyone with half a mind would think twice about trying to get past him.

Jake flashed his badge and the man

nodded at them and stepped aside as they approached the front door. Beth used her key to unlock it and then went inside.

The scent of smoke still lingered and the knot that was her heart tightened painfully. Hearing about the damage and actually seeing it were two different things.

The breakfast nook had been the focal point of the fire. The windows were gone, had exploded from the heat and the walls around the area were blackened. Still, it wasn't quite as bad as she'd imagined. The walls looked solid and the fire had been contained to the nook area.

Jake placed a large hand on her shoulder. "This will pass and all will be well again," he said.

She nodded, but she doubted that everything would ever be well again. She left the kitchen and went into the bedroom to pack a suitcase.

It was crazy, how in the space of three days Antoine had completely taken over her life, her heart. The fact that he'd told her he'd done terrible things as an interrogator for his country didn't taint the love she felt for him. It would be like blaming a soldier of war for having to kill his enemy in the middle of a battlefield.

The fact that he was tormented by what he'd had to do in the name of his country only spoke of the pure heart that beat in his magnificent chest.

When she had finished packing what she thought she needed for a couple of weeks away from the house, she and Jake got back into his car and returned to the hotel.

"We should have an official report on the fire within the next couple of days," Jake said. "Have you contacted your insurance agent yet?"

"Not yet. I'll do it sometime this afternoon," she replied.

"Beth, I don't know what your relationship is with Prince Antoine, but please take care of yourself. Bad things seem to happen around these royal visitors."

For a moment she had the urge to tell Jake everything, about the notes she'd found and about Aleksei Verovick, everything about

Antoine's suspicions that the attacks weren't about the COIN coalition at all but rather about something more personal.

But, she would be betraying Antoine's trust if she told, and besides she reminded herself that by this evening he'd know it all anyway. Jane's deadline was quickly approaching and there was no doubt that she would stick to her word and pass the notes to Jake that evening.

When they reached the hotel Jake lifted her suitcase from his trunk and insisted he walk her back to Antoine's suite.

Antoine opened the door and she saw the relief on his face. "Thank you, Sheriff," he said as Jake dropped the suitcase just inside the door.

"No problem," Jake replied. "I'll be in touch when I have more news and please, next time you decide to leave here, take your security with you or call me and I'll do my best to provide protection." With that Jake left and Beth turned to face Antoine.

"You can unpack your things in the

dresser," he said, "and there's plenty of room in the closet."

Beth shook her head. "I'm not staying here, Antoine."

His handsome features pulled into a deep frown. "Of course you're staying here," he replied with a touch of that natural command in his voice. "It's the only place I can ensure your safety."

"I'm going to stay in the hotel room where I was the other night. I have to get back to my real life, Antoine. I have duties and responsibilities here and I can't just hole up here with you and forget everything else."

He walked toward her, his eyes pleading. "Beth, please. My heart will only be at peace if you're here with me, where I know no more harm can come to you."

She took a step back, not wanting him to touch her in any way, afraid that he might be able to change her mind. What he didn't understand was that harm would come to her if she stayed here with him.

There was no doubt in her mind that they

would make love again, that he would make her fall deeper in love with him. Then there was a chance that her heart might start believing that somehow, someway, they had a future. And it would all be a lie, a fantasy that would never come true.

"I'll be fine here in the hotel," she replied. "We have a good security team and I feel safe here in the confines of the hotel."

"Have I done something wrong? Something to offend you?" he asked and then didn't wait for her to respond. "Beth, you're the most important woman in my life. I couldn't bear anything happening to you."

"Nothing will happen to me," she replied, a lump rising in the back of her throat. He was breaking her heart even now, telling her how important she was and yet unable to speak any words of love.

She picked up her suitcase and started for the door. "Beth?" he called and she turned back to look at him.

"The woman, Janine Sahron. Can you still arrange for me to speak to her?"

With everything that had transpired she'd

forgotten all about Janine. She glanced at her watch and then back at him. "Give me a little while to get settled into my room and then I'll go to the office and call her in. I'll let you know when she's there and you can speak with her."

"Thank you. Unfortunately, I only have the remainder of the afternoon before the notes will become public knowledge."

She nodded and then left the suite. She realized as crazy as it seemed, she'd wanted him to stop her from leaving, she'd wanted him to break down and tell her that he was madly, passionately in love with her and she'd completely changed his mind about never marrying, about never having a family of his own.

She was such a fool. Funny, she could swear that there had been moments when she'd felt not just red-hot passion, but also real love emanating from him.

And if she were perfectly honest with herself she'd admit that deep inside her was a crazy little niggle of hope that somehow, when this was all over, they would find a way to be together.

And that little bit of hope almost scared her as much as everything else that had happened in her life since she'd handed those notes over to Antoine.

Chapter Nine

She seemed to take the very air out of the suite when she left. Antoine eased down in the leather chair by the fireplace and stared toward the bank of windows, his thoughts consumed with Beth.

How had she managed in such a short space of time to do what no other woman had ever done before—get so deeply under his defenses?

As he imagined leaving this place and returning to Barajas without her in his life, his heart ached with a pain it had never felt before.

He loved her.

The knowledge blossomed inside of him. He wanted to wake up each morning with her head on the pillow next to his. He wanted to hear her laughter every day of his life. He needed to go to bed at night and hold her in his arms.

He loved her.

And he intended to do nothing about it.

He sighed wearily and leaned his head back. She deserved a man with no baggage, children whose safety she would never have to worry about, and a life filled with happiness and nothing else.

He couldn't give her that.

All he could give her was bad dreams and fear, a lifetime of wonder and worry, looking over her shoulder and wondering when somebody from his past might find them.

No matter how much he loved her, he would never allow her to have a meaningful place in his life. She meant far too much to him. The best thing he could do for her was let her go so she could find a man who could love her the way she was meant to be loved, a man who could give her a future filled with nothing but joy.

He stood as a knock sounded at his door.

It was Sheik Efraim Aziz. Antoine gestured the tall, dark-eyed man inside, grateful for the distraction from his thoughts.

"Would you like something to drink, my friend?" Antoine asked as Efraim sat on the sofa.

"No, I'm fine. I just wanted to check in, see how you were doing since your brother's return to Barajas."

Antoine eased down in the chair opposite Efraim. "Of course I miss him being here, but it was important that he return to Barajas and continue the job of running the country."

Efraim raked a hand through his black hair and released a sigh. "Who would have thought when we all got together and planned the COIN Coalition to benefit our nations that we would be sitting here now with one of us missing and betrayal surrounding us."

"You've learned nothing more from the other members of your security as to who Fahad might have been working with?"

Efraim frowned. "Nothing. The man

took his secrets to his grave and I'm still not sure who we can trust at the local law-enforcement level."

"What do you think of Sheriff Jake Wolf?" Antoine asked, aware that within hours Jake would have the notes Beth had found in his possession.

"He seems an honorable man, but Fahad certainly blindsided me and that makes me wary of trusting anyone."

Antoine offered his friend a small smile. "I hear there's one woman you've come to trust pretty well."

A responding smile curved Efraim's lips. "Callie." He said her name with warmth. "Yes, she has become important to me."

Callie McGuire was Assistant to the Secretary of Foreign Affairs based in Washington, D.C. She'd come to Wyoming to help facilitate the COIN summit. Her family owned a ranch locally and it had been on her land that Fahad had tried to kill Efraim. It had been Callie's brother who had killed Fahad when he'd believed his sister was in danger.

"From what I know of her, she seems to be a good woman," Antoine said.

"She is my heart," Efraim replied in a surprising show of emotion.

"I'm happy for you." Antoine felt the lump that formed in his throat as he thought of Beth and all that he would never share with her. "Do you plan to take her with you when you return home?"

"We have no plans beyond today," he replied. "Right now it's one day at a time, but whatever happens, wherever I go I know that she'll be at my side."

"Do you have any new theories about who was behind the attack on Amir?" Antoine asked, wanting to steer the conversation away from matters of the heart.

A frown once again swept across Efraim's features. "I have worked any number of theories in my brain, but can't make sense of any of them. I have thought about this until my head hurts and I can't come up with any definitive answers. What about you?"

"I wondered about Kalil Ramat."

Efraim's eyes widened. "We all know

the people of Saruk and Kalil himself were against the coalition, but we have all been guests at Kalil's home. His son is our friend. I can't imagine that Kalil would be behind a plot to kill us all."

Efraim only echoed what Antoine felt in his heart. "Beth Taylor, the head of housekeeping, found some notes in Amir's room taped to the bottom of a drawer." Antoine decided it was time to share what he knew.

"Notes?"

Antoine told Efraim what the notes contained and about he and Beth taking them to Jane for fingerprinting. "She managed to pull a print from them."

Efraim leaned forward in the chair, his features radiating a deadly calm. "Who?"

"A man named Aleksei Verovick. He has ties to the Russian mob."

"The mob would have no vested interest in us making trade agreements with the United States," Efraim scoffed. "What we need to do is find out who hired this Verovick."

"I agree. But that's easier said than done." Antoine released a weary sigh.

"You've given this information to Sheriff Wolf?"

"Not yet. He'll have the information tonight. If Verovick is here in town, then hopefully Wolf can find the man and get the answers we need."

"And find out what happened to Amir, although I must confess I fear the worst where he's concerned," Efraim said, his dark eyes filled with sadness. He stood. "I won't keep you any longer, I just wanted to see how things were going and if there were any developments since last we spoke."

Antoine walked him to the door, wishing he had the answers to who was behind all the attacks, and more importantly, what had happened to Amir. "We'll speak again soon," he said and clapped Efraim on the shoulder. "And we'll pray for our friend."

Efraim nodded and then left.

When he was gone Antoine walked to the

window and stood staring out at the Wyoming landscape that spoke to a place in his soul.

When would this all end? When would they finally have the answers they sought? Frustration burned inside his gut. If the Sahrons were somehow tied to Aleksei Verovick, then he would find out and they would finally have a trail to follow to the source.

And then, he would leave here and try his damndest to forget about a woman named Beth Taylor and the pieces of happiness she had given him.

When Beth finally called him he was ready. He felt a cold, hard resolve as he left his suite and headed to her office. He knew it was possible that Janine Sahron and her husband had nothing to do with anything that had been happening, but he needed to assure himself of that fact.

He knocked on the office door and his heart sang at the sound of Beth's voice bidding him entry. When he saw her he felt as if it had been days rather than a couple of hours since he'd last seen her.

He wondered if she knew that her smile let him know how deeply she'd grown to care about him. He tried to rein in his own emotions as he greeted her.

"Janine is on her way," she said as she sat behind the desk and gestured him into one of the two chairs in front of her. "You won't be too rough on her, will you? She seems to be a very nice woman."

"Then I'll keep the whips and chains hidden until I think we really need them," he said teasingly.

"Good, because I can't have that sort of thing happening in this nice resort. We do have a reputation to uphold, you know."

He was glad to see the teasing light in her eyes but once again he was reminded of all that he would never have with her.

At that moment a knock sounded at her door.

The woman who entered was a thin redhead with big blue eyes that instantly became guarded when she saw him. "You wanted to see me, Ms. Taylor?" A nervous twitch appeared at the corner of one of her eyes.

"Yes, Janine, please have a seat," Beth said. "This is Prince Antoine Cavanaugh. He'd like to ask you a few questions."

The nervous tick fluttered once again as she sank down on the chair. She nodded to Antoine and clutched her hands together in her lap and then looked back at Beth. "Is something wrong? Have I done something wrong with my work?"

"No, it's nothing like that," Beth quickly assured her. "Your work here has been exemplary." Janine seemed to relax a bit.

"Mrs. Sahron, I hope you don't mind me taking a few minutes of your time," Antoine said and gave her his most charming smile.

"Uh…no, I don't mind," Janine said.

Antoine could tell she was nervous not only by the eye twitch but also by the way her tongue slid over her lips, as if her mouth was unaccountably dry. It didn't mean she was guilty of anything. It was possible she was simply nervous because she was probably speaking to a prince for the first time in her life.

"Beth mentioned that your husband is from a Mediterranean island. Which one would that be?" he asked. He kept a light, easy tone to his voice.

"Nadar. Actually it's his parents who are from there. Hakim, my husband, was born here in the United States," she replied. The tick at the corner of her eye stopped and although her fingers remained laced together he noticed that some of the tension had dissipated.

"Ah, Nadar is a beautiful place. Do you visit there?" Antoine leaned back in his chair and looked at her as if he was interested in learning everything about her.

Her cheeks flushed slightly and she nodded. "We've gone to visit family there several times over the years. It is a beautiful place but it's expensive to travel."

"And what does your husband do here?" Antoine asked. He was aware of tension wafting from Beth, but he kept his focus on Janine, seeking any sign of deception in her body language.

"He's a math teacher, but during the summers he works at a video store to make some extra money. The house needs a lot of work." Once again she looked from Antoine to Beth. "Is something wrong? I'm afraid I don't understand…"

"I just hungered to speak with somebody from my area of the world," Antoine said and once again infused his smile with warmth. "What brought you and your husband to Dumont? I understand you've only recently moved to the area."

For the first time since she'd arrived in the room Janine unclasped her hands and leaned back in her chair and he knew she was starting to fully relax. "My grandparents are from Dumont. Five months ago they decided to go into an assisted-living facility and gifted Hakim and me their house. We were living in Texas, renting an apartment and trying to save up money for a house so it was like a gift from heaven." She was completely relaxed now, all signs of stress gone from her body language. "The house needs lots of work, so both Hakim and I are doing what we can to get extra money to make the repairs."

"Do you have sisters or brothers, Janine?" He leaned forward and gently touched her on the shoulder. She seemed to melt toward him.

"Two sisters," she replied.

"And you are very close to them, I can tell." He pulled his hand away from her shoulder but leaned into her, as if she were the most important person on the face of the earth.

A smile curved her lips. "Very close," she agreed.

"It's been a difficult couple of weeks for me," he said and saw the spark of sympathy that darkened her eyes. "I'm sure you've heard about the bombing of my friend Amir's car."

"Of course, everyone knows about it. It was a horrible thing that happened."

"He was a good friend to me…like my brother. If you'd heard anything about his whereabouts, if you had any clue as to who might have been behind the bombing, you would tell me, wouldn't you?"

Janine's eyes widened. "Of course. I'd want the people responsible brought to justice."

"And your husband? If he knew anything about it, he'd come forward to the authorities?"

Her brow crinkled in confusion. "Why would Hakim know anything about it? He knows about movies and math, but he doesn't know about what happens here at the resort unless I share it with him."

He believed her.

There were absolutely no signs of deception from her. If her husband was involved, then he was confident she had no idea about it.

"I appreciate you coming in to speak with me," he said as he stood. Just to be on the safe side he would give her husband's name to Jake Wolf and let him check out the man more thoroughly, but Antoine's gut instinct told him this was just another disappointing dead end.

Chapter Ten

Beth had watched him charm Janine, set her at ease with his warm, engaging smile and his gently orchestrated touch to her shoulder. A hard knot formed in the center of Beth's chest.

It was all so familiar, the way he'd manipulated her so easily.

Just like he'd manipulated Beth on the day she'd found the notes. She remembered that look in his eyes, the soft touch of his hand on her shoulder. Manipulation 101 and like Janine, Beth had fallen right in line and agreed to do whatever he wanted. And she'd continued to be manipulated by him.

He'd needed her. As Janine left the office Beth realized that the nice things Antoine had done for her, the caring she'd seen in his eyes, the passion she'd felt in his touch had probably all been a ruse to get what he wanted, what he needed from her.

That's what he did. That's what he'd been trained to do. He found weaknesses and exploited them and the biggest weakness she'd had was her aching loneliness and her overwhelming attraction to him.

"That was probably a waste of time," he said once Janine was gone. "I didn't detect any deception from her and my gut is telling me she doesn't know anything about Verovick or what's been happening."

"You're very good at what you do," she said as anger built up inside her.

He must have heard something in her tone for he closed the office door and then turned to face her once again. "I only asked her some questions."

"Oh, you did so much more than that." She remained on the other side of the desk as her anger continued to build. "That soft touch on the shoulder, that pain-filled gaze, so practiced and so effective at getting women to tell you whatever it is you want, to do whatever you need."

His eyes narrowed. "Beth, what is going on in that beautiful head of yours?"

"I think for the first time in days I'm finally seeing things clearly." She felt as humiliated and as stupidly naïve as she had when she'd found out that Mark was married. God, she'd been such a fool. He'd made her feel important, had acted like he was interested in every area of her life because he'd needed to use her to achieve his ultimate goals.

"And what is it that you think you're seeing clearly?" He walked toward her and she steeled herself not to allow her thoughts to get muddied by the familiar scent of him, by his very nearness.

"I was easy, wasn't I, Antoine. I was lonely and already had something of a crush on you. I was just ripe for the picking when it came to you finding somebody to use." To her horror hot tears burned at her eyes, but she swallowed hard against them, refusing to allow him to see her cry.

He stared at her in surprise. "Beth, you've got it all wrong," he said. He rounded the desk and reached for her, but she held up a hand to stop him before he could touch her in any way.

"Really? You didn't use manipulation and interrogation skills when you called me into your room the day I found those notes?" She gazed at him belligerently, daring him to lie to her.

His cheeks reddened slightly and he opened his mouth to speak and then paused as if he were collecting his thoughts. "Of course I did," he finally replied and the hard knot in her chest expanded.

"I knew that you'd found something in that room that was important and I wanted to know what it was," he continued. "Did I like what I had to do? Absolutely not. Did it have anything to do with what we've shared since then? Absolutely not."

She didn't believe him. She was afraid to believe him. Any crazy fantasy she'd entertained about them somehow having a future together had died a final death as she'd watched him talk to Janine.

It was over. Her heart had finally shut down. She refused to be a fool any longer. "Antoine, I think it best if we just say good-bye to each other here and now. You should call Jake and give him the information about the notes and your suspicions. I've done everything you needed and so there's really no reason for us to see each other anymore."

His eyes were the soft blue that beckoned her to fall into their depths, but she knew she'd be foolish to allow herself to give him the benefit of the doubt.

"Beth, not like this." His voice was a soft caress that only served to break her heart a little more. "I can't let this end with you thinking this has been nothing more than what I needed to help solve Amir's disappearance. It was about so much more."

"Please, just go," she said as new tears begged to be released.

Still he hesitated, as if wanting to say more and for a moment she imagined what she saw in his eyes was love, but then he took a step backward and gave her a stiff bow. "As you wish," he said and then turned on his heels and left the office.

The minute he was gone Beth sank down at her desk and allowed the tears to fall. She hadn't realized until now the tiny flare of ridiculous hope that had burned bright in her chest. And now it was gone and she was left feeling empty inside.

She hadn't really considered marriage to him, but she had desperately wanted to believe that when he'd made love to her it had been because he desired her to distraction and not because he'd needed to keep her on his side.

But, the truth of the matter was that he'd needed somebody who didn't have a stake in any of the intrigue that surrounded him. He'd told her again and again that he didn't trust the people around him. He'd needed a driver, a confidante, and she'd fit neatly into what he needed.

She could have been anyone…another maid, a member of room service or a clerk in the gift shop. And that's what hurt the most—that she could have been anyone whom he could manipulate into fitting what he needed.

She was grateful that nobody called or came into the office for the next hour; it took that long for her to shed the tears that had built up.

Antoine had been everything she ever wanted in a man. Her attraction to him had nothing to do with the fact that he was a prince. She'd loved him for his teasing sense of humor, for the soft heart she knew beat beneath his tightly muscled chest. She loved him for the way he'd made her feel—and that had been the biggest lie of all.

He'd warned her that he didn't want a wife, that he would never have a family. He'd at least been honest about that. And it was shame on her for thinking that what they had might make him forget his resolve to live alone for the rest of his life.

When her tears had finally been spent she went into the adjoining bathroom and fixed her makeup and at that moment her cell phone rang. She checked the ID and saw that it was Haley from the café.

"Hey, girl, sorry it's taken me so long to get back to you," Haley said.

"It's not a problem," Beth replied.

"You gave me a tall order," Haley continued. "I've been keeping an eye on the people who come in and I've got a couple of names for you."

"Hang on, let me get a pen and paper." Beth pulled a small notepad and pen from the desk. "I'm ready."

"The first name is Dimitri Petrov, he's a Russian who told me he's in town on business, but he was vague about what his business is. The second man told me his name is Abdul Jahard and that he's here in Dumont visiting relatives, but his relatives must not feed him because he's here for almost every meal. Unfortunately those are the only two I've identified as being slightly suspicious."

"How did you manage to get them to give you so much information about themselves?" Beth asked.

Haley laughed. "You know me, I could

get a rock to confess its sins to me if I had enough time. I just struck up a conversation with them while they were waiting for their orders."

"Thanks, Haley, I really appreciate it," Beth replied.

"Are you okay?"

"Sure, why?"

"I don't know, you sound kind of funny... sad."

Darn. Beth should have realized her friend would pick up on her emotional state just by talking to her. "I'm fine," she said and forced more life into her voice. "Just tired, that's all."

"We need to do lunch sometime soon," Haley said. "It's been too long."

"I'll call you and we'll set something up." With that the two disconnected. Beth wasn't interested in meeting for lunch too soon. She needed to get over the pain of Antoine before she felt like going anywhere with anyone.

She looked at the two names she'd written down. She'd finish her day and then she supposed she'd take the names to Antoine. A couple of hours wouldn't make any difference as to when he got the names from her. At the moment all she wanted to do was get back to the work of running her staff and spot-checking rooms.

She left her office but stayed away from the suites, not wanting to run into Antoine until she was better prepared to see him again. If he hadn't already contacted Jake Wolf about the notes she had found and the fingerprint that Jane had pulled, within hours Jane would be talking to the sheriff.

There was nothing more to be done. Even though Antoine feared there were dirty people working for the Sheriff, he had no choice but to give up the information. Maybe she'd just give the names Haley had given her to Jake. That way she wouldn't have to speak to Antoine again.

She could only hope that if Antoine remained here he would be safe. No matter how much her heart ached because of him, it was important to her that he stay well and return to his home to rule his nation with his twin brother.

It was after five when she finally grabbed her purse from the desk and decided to call it a night. She'd called her insurance agent while she'd waited for Antoine and Janine to come to her office and he'd assured her that they'd work to get her back into her house as soon as possible.

Hopefully if she and Antoine had nothing more to do with each other, then she could eventually go home without worrying about her own safety and all she'd have to deal with was her broken heart and the fact that she felt like she'd been played for a fool.

Once she got to her room she'd call Jake and give him the names of the two men Haley thought might be suspicious and then the intrigue with the visiting royalty and any connection to Antoine would be over for her.

As she left her office, she was plagued by an exhaustion deeper than anything she could ever remember feeling. It was an emotional weariness that she feared would be with her for a long time to come.

Being a fool for a man seemed to come naturally to her, she thought as she started across the lobby. It would be a long time before she put her heart on the line again for any man.

She was halfway across the lobby when a slightly overweight brunette waved from across the room and hurried toward her with a bright smile.

Beth racked her brain frantically in an effort to identify the woman. A former employee? A returning guest? She came up blank but forced a responding smile as the woman reached her.

"Beth…Beth Taylor?" Faint shadows darkened the skin beneath her brown eyes, as if she hadn't been sleeping well.

Beth steeled herself, wondering if there was a complaint coming over the quality of the pillows or the bedding or any number of other things that could keep a guest from sleeping well. "Yes, I'm Beth," she replied. "May I help you?"

The woman took a step closer, invading Beth's personal space. "Yes, you can help me, but more importantly you can help Prince Antoine and the other royals staying at the hotel."

Beth froze, her heart suddenly pounding a thousand beats a minute. "What are you talking about?" she asked in a half-whisper.

"Keep smiling, Beth," the woman said, her eyes like hard brown pebbles. "I've planted a bomb in the prince's suite and all I have to do to detonate it is flip this little switch." She opened her hand to show Beth what looked like a remote control of some kind.

Everything in the lobby faded away as Beth struggled to make sense of what she'd just said. A bomb? In Antoine's suite? "What do you want?"

"You have your car keys?"

Beth gripped her purse tightly and nodded. She wished there was a gun inside her purse instead of her keys, some lipstick and her cell phone.

"You're going to walk nice and slowly

toward the door and we're going to get into your car." The smile never left the woman's lips. "If you move too fast, I'll push the button. If you try to get anyone else's attention or do anything at all, I'll blow the roof off this place. Do you understand?"

Beth wasn't sure if she nodded or not, but she must have for the woman nodded with satisfaction. "Good," she said. "Let's go."

Beth didn't know about bombs. She had no idea if this woman was lying, but she couldn't take that chance. She couldn't put Antoine's life at risk. Or anyone else's.

"Move it," the woman said, her voice rough despite the fact her smile never faltered.

Beth felt as if she were in a horrible dream as her feet moved her across the lobby toward the front door. They had considered the Russian mob, they'd worried about Antoine's security team and the local law officials. But, nobody had told her to be worried about an overweight brunette with tired brown eyes.

"YOU SHOULD HAVE brought these to me immediately when Beth found them." Jake Wolf was not a happy man.

Antoine had left Beth and come directly to his suite, more upset than he could ever remember being. But, instead of dwelling on what had just happened with Beth, he'd immediately called the sheriff to meet him.

"At the time that the notes were found I wasn't sure who I could trust," Antoine replied. "And that included any local law enforcement."

"Even if you didn't trust me or my men, you could have taken them to the federal agents who have been working this case," Jake replied as he sat on the sofa.

"I know less about them than I do about you and your men," Antoine replied. "There was no way I was going to give them what I thought might be vital information."

Jake released a weary sigh and laid the copy of the notes he'd just read on the ornate coffee table before him. "When I became sheriff I inherited a corruption that had been in the ranks for years. Payoffs for a variety of things were common and I swore that I'd clean things up. Unfortunately, it's not done yet. I'm still working on it."

Antoine didn't know if he was a fool or not, but he trusted the man in front of him. Or maybe it was just the fact that he now found himself in a position where he was forced to trust him.

"In any case, Beth and I took the notes to Jane and she was able to lift a print that belonged to Aleksei Verovick." As he told the sheriff everything he had learned about the man, he tried to keep thoughts of Beth at bay.

He didn't want to think about the yawning pain he'd seen in her eyes, the utter sense of betrayal that had laced her tone. She'd been shattered by what she believed had been his lies and manipulations. Like one of the military criminals he'd once interrogated, he'd broken Beth.

"When I get back to my office I'll begin a search for this Verovick. If he's here in town I'll know about it," Jake said, his features hard with resolve. "Is there anything else you've been holding back from me?"

"No, that's it. And I apologize for not bringing the notes to you sooner." In trying to investigate on his own he had only managed to put Beth's life at risk and break her heart.

Jake pulled himself up from the couch. "I'll see what I can do with this and be in touch."

"Thank you, I appreciate it." He followed Jake to the door. "I was desperate to see if I could find out anything about Amir's disappearance. I had hoped he was still alive, but with each day that passes my hope gets more difficult to maintain."

Jake's eyes grew darker. "I hope we get some closure where Sheik Amir is concerned," he replied, but Antoine knew by his tone of voice that he, too, was having difficulty maintaining any real hope that Amir was still alive.

Once Jake had left, Antoine paced the living area of the suite, his thoughts once again on Beth. He figured he'd give her a little while to cool off and then he'd try to speak to her again.

He couldn't allow her to believe that she'd been nothing but a pawn for him to manipulate and use and then discard when he was finished with her.

She'd been so much more than that and he needed to make her understand. The weight of what he'd done to her coupled with his own heartbreak nearly crippled him.

He needed her to understand that she deserved more than he could ever give her, that he loved her but sometimes love wasn't enough to overcome life's obstacles.

He finally threw himself in the leather chair and buried his face in his hands. There was nothing worse than to love a woman and be unable to allow her fully into your life.

Beth was everything he wanted, everything he needed. She was the woman he wanted beside him every day of his life, the woman who made him want to be a better man. But he'd made a vow to himself long ago and he couldn't, he wouldn't make the mistake his father made.

Perhaps it was best that she was angry and felt completely betrayed by him. Maybe this was the kindest way to end their relationship.

He held on to that thought until he could stand it no longer and then he grabbed his cell phone and called her. He couldn't allow it to end this way, with her thinking she had been stupid to believe in him and had meant nothing to him.

Her phone rang three times and then went to voice mail. She was probably screening her calls and didn't want to talk to him. He tried a second time with the same result and then returned his cell phone to his pocket and decided to go in search of her.

He could not let it end this way. Somehow he had to make her understand that she hadn't been the fool, but perhaps he was.

He left the suite and headed for her office, hoping she would still be there despite the fact that it was just after five.

She wasn't in. He drifted back to the

lobby, sickened with the overwhelming need to make things right with her, to somehow make her understand that he hadn't been using her.

He peeked into the coffee shop area, wondering if maybe she was getting a bite to eat, but she was nowhere in sight and he had no idea what room she was staying in here at the hotel. He also wasn't at all sure that anyone who worked at the hotel would give him that information.

He smiled as he approached one of the young, attractive women working the front desk. Her name tag read Julia. "Ms. Julia," he said in greeting.

"Prince Antoine," she replied with a touch of breathlessness. She was little more than a teenager and Antoine had a feeling she was not only intimidated by his presence, but also more than a little bit tickled. "How can I help, Your Majesty?"

If he hadn't been so worried about Beth, he might have found her grandiose title humorous. "I was looking for Ms. Taylor. Have you seen her recently?"

"Beth Taylor? She left for the day," the girl replied.

"Yes, I checked her office and I know she's gone from there, but I also know she's staying in a room here in the hotel and I really need to speak with her."

"Is this a housekeeping issue?" she asked. "I'm sure I can find somebody else for you to speak with if there's a problem."

"No problem," he replied smoothly. "And it's a personal issue."

"I'm afraid I can't help you. Ms. Taylor left the hotel a few minutes ago."

Antoine stared at her, certain that he must have heard her incorrectly. "What?"

"I saw her leave just a little while ago." She pointed toward the front doors.

Antoine's heart began a rapid beat. Why would Beth leave the hotel? She knew there was danger outside. She'd told him she was going to stay in a room here at the hotel. "Was she alone when she left?"

Julia frowned. "I think she was with another woman."

Another woman? His mind raced with

suppositions as he left the desk and hurried to the front door. Once there he checked the parking lot and saw that her Jeep was gone.

Why would she leave the hotel and who had she left with? Although there was no real reason to panic, that's exactly what he felt—a screaming alarm that something wasn't right.

He hurried back to his suite, his heart pounding as fast as his footsteps clicking against the marble floor. Once he got inside his suite he powered up his laptop, grateful that he'd thought about having the tracking device placed on her car.

Her Jeep was on the move, but it was not going toward her home, rather it appeared to be headed into an area where he thought from his trips back and forth to her place that there was nothing but woods.

He stared at the monitor screen as the alarm in his head screamed louder. She was in trouble. He had absolutely no facts to support his belief, but every instinct he possessed told him she was in danger.

He yanked his cell phone from his pocket

and dialed Michael. "Get David to bring the car and meet me at the front door immediately," he said to his head security man.

"Yes, sir," Michael replied without question.

Antoine grabbed his laptop and raced out of the suite, a frantic anxiety clawing at his insides. It made no sense. It made no sense at all that she would have left the hotel, that she would be heading into an area where there was nothing but wilderness.

He'd headed into battle many times over the years, but never feeling as if so much was at stake. When he ran out the front doors, David, his driver, had the car pulled against the curb with Michael riding shotgun.

Antoine slid into the backseat and slammed the door. "Beth Taylor is in trouble. We must get to her before it's too late." He handed Michael his laptop over the seat. "Find her. We have to get to her."

David looked at the screen, put the car into gear and headed for the hotel exit.

"What kind of danger are we facing?"

Michael asked, his tone clipped and all business as he pulled his gun from his shoulder holster.

"I don't know. I only know she shouldn't have left the hotel. She knew she might be in danger if she ventured out and she's not a foolish woman. The woman behind the desk said she left with another woman."

"Could she not just be going with a friend for dinner or something?" Michael asked.

Antoine gestured toward the computer screen impatiently. "And where will they find food in the middle of nowhere?" He shook his head. "I feel it in my gut, Michael. She's in trouble."

"We'll find them," David said as he stepped on the gas. They couldn't go fast enough to ease the burn in Antoine's stomach.

It was Antoine's worst nightmare come true. He was certain that somebody from his past had taken Beth and they were going to make her pay for all his sins.

Chapter Eleven

"Who's paying you to do this?" Beth asked, trying not to lose it because the woman now no longer just held the remote control, but also a gun.

"Shut up," she snapped. "Slow down and turn in between those two trees on the right where there's a little trail."

Beth held the steering wheel so tight her fingers cramped. There had been a dozen times in the last five minutes of driving she'd thought about bailing out of the car, but she was afraid of that remote control, afraid that any wrong move on her part would mean Antoine's death.

And as if that wasn't worry enough, there was the problem of the gun in the woman's hand and the deadly intent in her eyes. She looked like somebody who wouldn't hesitate to pull the trigger.

Beth made the turn the woman had indicated and had to bring the car to a halt because of the grove of trees in front of them. The area was isolated with overgrown brush and thick trees crowding together.

The woman next to her seemed nervous. Beth noticed that her hands shook slightly and she chewed her bottom lip. That was the only thing that gave Beth a little bit of hope…that somehow she might be able to talk her way out of this mess.

"He won't care, you know," she said. "If you kill me he'll still eventually follow through and make trade agreements with the United States."

"I told you to shut up," the woman screamed, as if she were hanging on to her control by a very thin thread. "Get out of the car and don't be stupid. If you're stupid then I'll shoot you and blow him to smithereens."

Tears blurred her vision as Beth got out of the car. She had no idea what this woman intended, but it couldn't be good. They were in a wilderness area, where nobody would hear Beth scream, where nobody would blink at the sound of a gunshot.

Nobody knew where she had gone. She wasn't even sure anyone would know that she'd left the hotel. She was in deep trouble and she knew she could only depend upon herself to get out of it.

As the woman punched the barrel of the gun in the small of her back and ordered her to walk, Beth knew she had to be patient and wait for the perfect opportunity, pray that the perfect opportunity would come and she'd be able to take the woman down without getting killed in the process.

As they continued to walk deeper into the woods, Beth began to realize that she'd probably been a fool…again. She knew nothing about bombs, but she was beginning to think that there was no way a remote control could blow up the suite considering the distance they had traveled from the resort.

Still, she now had to worry about the gun

and her own life. Was this woman somehow tied to Antoine's past? Was she seeking revenge against him? Was she a part of Antoine's nightmares?

She cried out as she stumbled over a fallen tree and fell to her knees. The woman grabbed her by the arm and yanked her up, muttering curses beneath her breath.

"Keep moving," she said as she once again pressed the gun painfully into Beth's back.

Beth felt as if they walked for hours, but in reality knew that it had probably been less than an hour since she'd made what might turn out to be a fatal mistake by walking out of the resort.

How she wished she could replay that moment when the woman had walked up to her in the lobby. How she wished she would have taken a risk and signaled for security instead of foolishly allowing herself to be put in the position she was in now.

The deeper they walked into the woods, the more the woman muttered unintelligibly beneath her breath. Maybe she was some crazy extremist, Beth thought. She definitely appeared unstable, but Beth didn't know if that was to her advantage or would ultimately work against her.

There was an unnatural silence in their surroundings, as if all of the woodland creatures sensed the danger that had entered their midst and held their breath in fear.

They finally reached a small clearing. "Stop," the woman said. "Turn around."

Beth slowly turned to find the gun now directed at the center of her body. "Are you working for the Russian mob?" Beth asked. She had to somehow make the woman talk. She needed to know who had hired the woman for her own sake, but more important she needed to buy herself some time to find a weakness and somehow exploit it.

The woman's eyes darted around the area and then settled back on Beth. "This is perfect. Nobody will ever find you here."

"Is this where you brought Amir? Is he buried somewhere in this clearing?" Beth didn't think her heart could beat any faster than it already was, but as she thought of the missing Sheik's body being buried in a grave in the clearing, it beat even faster.

The woman frowned and took a step back from Beth. "I don't know Amir and the only body who will be buried in this clearing is yours."

"Please, don't do this," Beth said, her heart once again fluttering frantically in her chest. "Whatever you want, whatever you need, killing me isn't the answer." Tears misted her vision as she thought about never seeing Antoine again, about not living long enough to find true love, to have children and to achieve the dreams she'd always wanted.

"I have to kill you," the woman screamed once again. The gun trembled in her hand, but didn't sway enough from Beth's center for her to make a move.

"You have to be gone," she continued. "It's the only way, the only way things will be better."

Beth tensed, waiting for the perfect opportunity to leap forward and wrestle for control of the gun. "How does killing me make things better?"

"Because he'll stop thinking about you, because he'll finally stop loving you." The woman spat the words as her features twisted with a rage that nearly took Beth's breath away.

"Antoine doesn't love me," Beth exclaimed.

"Not him, you stupid bitch. Mark!"

The frantic beat of Beth's heart paused as she stared at the woman. Mark? Mark Ferrer? "Who are you?" The question fell from her lips on a whisper even though in her heart she knew the answer.

"I'm Karen, you stupid cow. Karen Ferrer. I'm his wife, the woman who had his children. I'm the one who takes care of him, who loves him and you ruined it all!"

A hysterical burst of laughter rose to Beth's lips, but she quickly swallowed it down. They had been so worried that somebody from Antoine's past might use her to get to him. But, the real threat hadn't been somebody from his past…it had been somebody from hers.

THEY FOUND THE JEEP PARKED in a stand of trees and Antoine's heart leapt into his throat when he realized the vehicle was empty.

"What now?" Michael asked.

"We go hunting until we find her." Antoine got out of the car along with Michael. "David, you stay here with the car ready in case she's been hurt, and call Jake Wolf, tell him where we are and to get out here as soon as possible."

Antoine pulled his gun and looked at Michael who also had his gun at the ready. Which way? Antoine scanned the area carefully, seeking signs that the brush had been disturbed, that the grass had been tamped down by footsteps. Tension held him so tight he felt as if he might snap at any minute.

He knew if he didn't pick the right direction they would lose precious minutes…

minutes that could mean Beth's death—if he wasn't already too late.

He mentally shook himself, refusing to allow his thoughts to go there. She had to be okay. He steadfastly refused to believe otherwise. He knew that if she wasn't he'd be forever destroyed.

Seeing some tall grass that looked slightly trampled, he motioned for Michael to follow him, praying that they were going in the direction that would take him to Beth.

As they moved with the silence of ghosts through the woods, Antoine wondered who in the hell had gotten to her, which of his enemies had managed to get her from the hotel and into these woods? What possible ruse could they have used to get Beth to walk out of the hotel?

Julie had indicated that she thought Beth had left with a woman. How clever. Beth would have never considered going anywhere with a man she didn't know, but a woman? Perhaps using some sort of a sob story?

God, part of what he loved about Beth

was her trusting nature and it was possible that was the trait that might bring her to her death. He tightened his grip on his gun. He could shoot a woman as easily as he could a man if she intended to harm Beth.

Every few steps he motioned for Michael to halt and they listened for any sounds of other human presence in the woods. There was nothing, no noise to indicate there was either human or beast nearby.

The only sound Antoine could hear clearly was the frantic beating of his own heart. He'd done this to her. He'd brought danger to her doorstep and he'd never forgive himself if he'd ultimately gotten Beth killed.

They walked for what seemed like forever when Antoine thought he heard the faint sound of a voice coming from up ahead. He raised his hand to Michael and they stopped. Antoine strained to listen and his heart leaped as again he thought it was a female voice he heard.

He leaned toward Michael. "No sudden moves," he whispered. "We need to assess the situation before either of us makes a move."

Michael nodded and together the two men moved forward. The voice grew louder and after several more steps Antoine saw a clearing ahead and what stood in the clearing made his heart nearly stop beating.

Beth stood facing a woman Antoine had never seen before, holding a gun pointed directly at Beth. He noticed several things instantly—Beth's terror showed in the strain of her features and he could easily imagine the tick firing off in the side of her slender neck, a neck he wanted to save.

The woman with the gun was nervous. She shifted her weight from foot to foot as her hand trembled. Antoine knew her nervousness made her even more dangerous.

"You ruined my life," the woman screamed. "We were happy and in love until you came along."

"I didn't know he was married," Beth exclaimed, her voice filled with her fear. "I haven't seen him or talked to him for almost a year."

Antoine frowned as his mind raced. This wasn't somebody who was after him, this was somebody seeking revenge against Beth.

Mark Ferrer's wife. The name of the man who hurt Beth was emblazoned on Antoine's brain. Antoine could only imagine the emotions raging inside the woman. It was obvious she believed that Beth had destroyed her marriage, ruined her life.

"You're lying," she screamed at Beth. "I knew something was wrong with him for a long time and finally a week ago he confessed that he'd had an affair with you, that he'd tried to break it off but you were obsessed with him."

It was obvious Mark Ferrer had lied to his wife, but it was equally obvious his wife wasn't going to believe anything Beth said.

As she grabbed the gun with both hands and steadied herself, Antoine knew he only had seconds to act. He shoved his gun in the back of his waistband and stepped out into the clearing. "Mrs. Ferrer."

She jumped and thankfully didn't shoot,

but she whirled the gun in his direction. He immediately raised his hands to show her that he didn't have a weapon.

"Don't come any closer," she yelled. She pointed the gun back at Beth. "If you come closer I'll shoot her."

The woman's brown eyes were huge and filled with a combination of rage and fear and more than a little bit of crazy.

"I won't come any closer," Antoine said in a gentle tone. "I just want to speak with you, that's all." He knew that Michael had his gun pointed at the woman's head, that if Michael sensed any imminent danger to Antoine he'd kill the woman without blinking an eye. But, Antoine hoped he could save both women who were suffering from the same fate—broken hearts.

"Mrs. Ferrer...can I call you by your first name?" he asked.

She stared at him as if he was the one who had lost his mind. "Karen," she finally said with a shrug of her shoulders. "My name is Karen."

"Karen, I'm Antoine." He forced what

he hoped was a charming smile to his lips. "Karen, I'm so sorry you've been having a rough time lately."

Her narrow lips trembled and tears sprang to her eyes. "You have no idea. Everything has been broken. She broke it!"

"I know. She was a selfish fool to mess with your husband," Antoine said smoothly. He kept his gaze focused solely on Karen and away from Beth. "It was you who tried to burn down her house?"

"She deserved to lose her house after she ruined my marriage. I ran her off the road, too." Her entire body shook with fury. "I would have made her pay that day but the two of you managed to get away from me."

"You said you have children? How many?" He needed to try to defuse some of the rage that made her entire body tremble.

A softness swept over her features. "Three. Jason is six, Matthew is four and Angela is three." The last of her words choked out of her on a sob. "We were a family, a happy family until she came along." The gun wavered and Antoine took the opportunity to take a step closer. "We were a family until she came along," she cried again, tears streaking down her cheeks.

"And you believe that if she's out of the way then you can be a family again," he replied.

"Yes! She has to leave him alone. She has to go away," Karen exclaimed and once again focused the gun on Beth.

"If you kill her then you'll go to jail, Karen. What about your children? Who will raise them while you're in prison?" Antoine took yet another step closer to the obviously distraught woman.

"Karen, let me help you," he continued, keeping his voice as soft, as non-threatening as possible. "I can make her go away. I'm the prince of a Mediterranean island. I can take her there and make sure she never returns to the States, that she never bothers you again."

At that moment hope flared in her eyes and she let down her guard. The tip of the gun lowered toward the ground and Antoine sprang.

Too late, his brain screamed as he saw the gun rise once again and point at Beth. Everything seemed to happen in slow motion. In his peripheral vision he saw a blur and at the same time he yelled Beth's name as the gun exploded.

He tackled Karen to the ground and wrestled the gun from her hand. Screaming and cursing, she fought him, but he easily got her under control.

A glance in Beth's direction nearly stopped his heart. A rush of relief whirled through him as he saw her still standing, but the relief was short-lived as he saw Michael on the ground at her feet.

At that moment his driver, David, arrived and Antoine thrust the still-cursing Karen at him. "Take her to the car," Antoine said, his gaze going to Beth who had crumpled to the ground next to the fallen Michael. As David took control of Karen, Antoine rushed forward and fell to his knees at Michael's side.

"I'm all right," Michael said as he struggled to sit up. He gripped his upper arm where a stain of blood had begun to appear on his shirt. "I think it's just a flesh wound."

Antoine helped him to his feet as sirens sounded in the distance. "Can you make it back to the car?" he asked. "It sounds like help is on the way."

Michael nodded and took off walking in the direction of the car. Antoine turned back to Beth, who was still on the ground and weeping softly into her hands.

It was only then that the complete relief began to wash over Antoine. She was safe. Thank God, she was safe. He crouched down next to her, wanting desperately to take her into his arms, but afraid of overstepping his boundaries considering what had taken place between them in her office.

"It's over," he said gently.

She dropped her hands from her face and gazed at him with tear-washed eyes. "She said she had a bomb planted in your suite and if I didn't come with her she'd blow it up. I thought maybe she was telling the truth and I couldn't take the chance that she'd hurt you."

Her words tumbled over themselves as her tears continued to flow. "I thought maybe she was working for the Russian mob, or maybe she was some kind of fanatic trying to stop the trade agreements. And then she had the gun and I knew there was no way for me to get away from her."

He could stand it no longer. He pulled her up and she came willingly into his arms and buried her face in the front of his shirt as he held her tight.

He closed his eyes, unable to believe how close he'd come to losing her. If it hadn't been for Michael the shot might have found Beth. He would never doubt Michael's trustworthiness again.

They were still standing in each other's arms when Jake Wolf and several of his men arrived. Jake shook his head as he approached them. "You two hotshots seem to be keeping me busy lately."

Beth stepped out of Antoine's arms and he felt not only the bereavement of her physical nearness, but her mental connection as well.

The danger was over and he realized they were back to where they'd been when he'd walked out of her office earlier in the day. He and Michael had managed to save her life, but nothing had really changed.

The night was endless. They all convened at Jake's office and statements were taken. Michael was treated and released with a bandage over his wound of courage and Karen was locked up to await trial on kidnapping and attempted murder charges.

When they were finally free to go, Antoine and Beth walked out of the building side by side. They had scarcely spoken to each other after Jake had arrived and throughout the long hours of interrogation.

During that time Antoine had reached a painful decision. As she headed for her Jeep in the parking lot he stopped her by taking hold of her arm.

In the illumination from the parking lot lights overhead he could see the weariness on her face, that faint pulse in the side of her throat and a raw vulnerability that would forever haunt him.

She pulled away from him, as if his very touch hurt her. He dropped his arms to his sides and fought his need to pull her to him and hold her close, hold her until she no longer fought him, until he'd convinced her of what she meant to him.

"I'll be returning to Barajas in the morning," he said.

She looked at him in surprise. "I thought you were staying until there was news about Amir."

"I'll leave the investigation in Jake's capable hands. I haven't been successful in helping anything. It's time I go home, but before I leave it's important to me that you understand that it was real, the emotions I feel for you are real and deep. I told you that I would never marry, but I will carry the memory of you with me for the rest of my life."

She studied him for a long moment. "You don't have to worry about your enemies finding you to get revenge." The pain in her eyes became sadness.

He frowned, confused by her words. "What do you mean?"

"They've already gotten their revenge on you. You will forever be alone because you fear what they might do, what might happen."

She released a weary sigh. "We all have things in our past, Antoine. Tonight was a perfect example that danger can come from unexpected places and people. You can get hit by a car, or get a terminal illness. It's what you do with the life you're given that's important, not the things you don't do because you're afraid."

She didn't wait for his response but instead turned on her heels and headed for the Jeep in the distance. He remained frozen in place as she got into the vehicle and then a moment later disappeared into the darkness of the night.

At eight-thirty the next morning Antoine

and his entourage were at the airport where the private jet was being readied for departure.

As they waited Antoine turned to Michael. "It will be good to get home," he said, as if the words themselves would be enough to convince him.

"I've had enough Wyoming to last me a lifetime," Michael replied.

Antoine studied the man for a long moment. "Your job has always been to protect me from harm. Why did you risk your life by throwing yourself in front of Beth?"

Michael met his gaze evenly. "Because I knew how important she was to you."

Antoine swallowed around the lump that rose in the back of his throat. He had spent most of the night trying not to think about Beth, telling himself that the best thing he could do was return to Barajas and put his time in this beautiful state of America behind him.

He needed to forget the woman who had stood by his side through danger, kissed him with a passion that had stirred his very soul and made him think of dreams that could never be his.

"It's time to board," Michael said as one of the men on the tarmac motioned to them.

Antoine nodded, straightened his shoulders and headed for the plane.

BETH SAT AT HER DESK in her office and stared out the window. This morning the events of the night before seemed like nothing more than a bad dream.

Amir was still missing, Karen was in jail and Antoine was now winging his way back to where he belonged. It was time for her to put the last week away in her mind, in a place where it couldn't be accessed and create any more pain.

"Easier said than done," she muttered under her breath. She turned away from the window and looked at the inventory list in front of her.

For a moment her body recalled every moment of being in Antoine's arms. Her skin warmed with the memory and a wistful sigh brought the sting of tears to her eyes.

Funny, but in the brief conversation they'd had in the parking lot at the sheriff's office, she'd believed him. She'd believed that she had been more to him than somebody to use and then discard at will.

Even a man as good as Antoine was at manipulation couldn't have manufactured the look of love in his eyes when he'd gazed at her and didn't know she saw him. She'd tasted the desire in his kisses, felt the caring in his touch and had finally believed in her heart that he had loved her.

A lot of good it did either of them. He was a man tied to a tragic past that wouldn't allow him to move forward, a man who would forever be trapped by what he considered the sins of his father.

And what had his father done? Simply loved a woman, loved her enough to put his fears behind him and risk everything for that love.

Time for her to get back to her real life,

she thought as she once again tried to focus her thoughts on the paperwork in front of her.

Fifteen minutes later a knock was heard on her door. "Come in," she said. The door opened and for a long moment she stared, mouth agape at Antoine.

"You can't be here," she said in confusion. "You're on your way back to Barajas." He looked so incredibly handsome in a military jacket covered with metals and ribbons. He looked every inch the prince that he was and her heart squeezed tight.

She stood, her legs feeling ridiculously weak. "What are you doing here?"

He walked over to the window and stared out with his back to her. She held on to the edge of the desk, wondering what was going on, why he was prolonging her agony by attempting to speak to her again.

When she thought she might scream with anxiety, he turned and looked at her. "I had every intention of returning to Barajas this morning. I got to the airport where my plane was waiting and told myself it was what I wanted to do, what I needed to do. But, when it came time to actually get on the plane, I couldn't."

He stepped away from the window and walked close enough to her that she could smell that dizzying cologne of his, see the silver shards that glinted in his pale blue eyes.

"I never wanted to rule Barajas. Sebastian is much better suited for the role of leadership. I've discovered that I've fallen in love with Wyoming. The land speaks to me and whispers that this is the place where I belong."

Is this what he'd come to tell her? That he intended to make a home here in Wyoming? In Dumont? God, the idea of running into him at the grocery store, seeing him on the streets was horrifying. How could she forget him if he was right here under her nose? It would have been so much better if he'd gone back to his island.

"You don't look happy," he said.

She mentally shook herself and pasted on a smile. "I want you to be happy, Antoine, and if you find happiness here then I'm glad for you."

His gaze seemed to pierce right through her as he took a step closer. "I've also been thinking a lot about what you said to me last night."

"Oh?" The word froze in her throat as he began to unbutton the dress military jacket.

"I think if I had the opportunity to ask my father if he had any regrets about loving my mother, about making her his wife, he'd tell me no. And my mother would have no regrets either. I remember their love for each other and know that even if they knew what the future held for them, they would have chosen to have the years that they did of love and family together."

She stared at him, her breath caught in her chest, afraid to try to guess where this all might lead.

"The past can be a tricky thing, Beth. It can bring you enormous joy or it can cage you like an animal at the zoo. I've been caged for a very long time." He shrugged off the jacket, exposing a white shirt beneath. He dropped the jacket to the floor and stepped so close to her she could feel the heat of his body warming hers.

"You take my breath away, Beth Taylor. For you I want to bend the bars of my cage and break free. I want to rebuild your house and make it big enough for a family. I love you, Beth, and I want to stay here with you and raise children and horses and embrace the happiness I know my parents would want for me."

Joy blossomed inside her, a joy that brought tears to her eyes as she threw herself into his arms. He wrapped her in a tight embrace that felt like love, that felt like safety, but more importantly felt like home.

"Antoine, I love you with all my heart, with all my soul," she said.

He released a sigh of sweet contentment and smiled. "You know that when we marry, you'll become a princess."

"I don't care about that," she replied. "Just being ordinary rancher Antoine Cavanaugh's wife is more than enough for me."

"Then I think we should go to the suite and start practicing to make the babies that you want," he said as his hands cupped her buttocks and pulled her even closer against him.

"Impertinent," she exclaimed, "definitely impertinent."

He laughed and his eyes blazed as his lips found hers and took them in a kiss that promised everything Beth had ever dreamed of, a kiss that spoke of love and passion and forever.

* * * * *

Don't miss
SOVEREIGN SHERIFF
by Cassie Miles
when COWBOYS ROYALE *continues.*
Look for it wherever
Harlequin Intrigue books are sold!

LARGER-PRINT BOOKS!

GET 2 FREE LARGER-PRINT NOVELS PLUS
2 FREE GIFTS!

⬥ Harlequin®

INTRIGUE®

BREATHTAKING ROMANTIC SUSPENSE

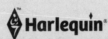